- THE GALILEO PROJECT – Part 2: COUNTDOWN

By

Si Rosser

Schmall World Publishing

First published in Great Britain as an e-book by Schmall World Publishing

Sirosserauthor.com

STOP! Have you read the first book in the series yet?
The Galileo Project: Part 1

"While working with a camera crew supervising flight testing of advanced aircraft at Edward's Air Force Base, California, the camera crew filmed the landing of a strange disc object that flew in over their heads and landed on a dry lake nearby. A camera crewman approached the saucer; it rose up above the area and flew off at a speed faster than any known aircraft."

-- Astronaut Gordon Cooper

CHAPTER 1

Welsh Mountains, U.K.

Present Day

ROBERT SPIRE DIPPED his head against the biting wind as he continued along the steep route up to the summit of Pen-y-Fan, which rose to a height of 886 metres above sea level in the Brecon Beacons mountain range. Not a hard mountain to climb, unless you were unfit, but no stroll in the park either. The SAS still used the range as a training ground, which meant it was a small achievement to climb up if nothing else.

A week had passed since Professor Lazarus' assassination and the subsequent meeting at GLENCOM. Spire had been unable to sleep properly since then, his mind racing with the details of the presentation given by Lazarus and also the talk that UFO historian, Dr Richard Doman, who'd travelled over at the drop of a hat from the United States, had given. It had been a very interesting briefing on the UFO phenomenon and Spire had been seeing little green men in his sleep since, hence the need to get out here, in the middle of nowhere to try and clear his mind, and get some much needed exercise.

He continued up the slow uphill ascent past the forestry plantation, the winding footpath easily negotiable, but the weather getting worse the higher he went, unbelievable for mid-August. Well, not that unbelievable he told himself, he was in Wales, U.K. after all.

As he trudged up, two men slowly overtook him and gave him a brief nod to acknowledge him as he let them pass. They both had pony tails, one of the men carrying two flag poles. Kind of odd, Spire thought.

The path up to the top of the mountain was about four feet wide, the mountain rising up on his right and dropping off to the fern-covered valley and stream below. Normally the views would be awe-inspiring; over to his left was the Cwm Llwch valley, and nestled in the bottom, Llyn Cwm Llwch, the legendary river and wonderful example of the valley's upland glacial moraine, but today Spire couldn't see any of it. Spire continued up, smiling to himself at the Welsh name for the mountain, Pen y Fan, which simply means, *the mountain's peak* – which didn't sound quite so dramatic, Spire considered. The mountain's secondary summit, was previously named, Cadair Arthur – *King Arthur's Chair*. Legend has it that the king once helped the people of Brecon who were being terrorised by a pack of wild boars. Once the king had killed the pack leader, the body of the boar rolled down into a river, which today is known as Afon Twrch, *or river of the boar*. True or not, the information Spire had gleaned about the mountain added some mystic to it.

Despite being an accessible peak for hikers of any level, it is considered to be one of the most dangerous mountains in Wales due to the changeable weather conditions that came with it, and Spire now realised why; dry and mild weather when he started off, but now horizontal rain and a gale blasting him from all directions.

He continued up, mulling last weeks' events over in his mind, and the most recent news on the Corona outbreak. There had been some good news in that regard at least. Major drug companies had just announced successful vaccine trials which boded well for eradication of the Covid-19 virus six months or so from now.

Spire's thoughts were dragged back to the assassination of Lazarus and of the bizarre message left by the professor for Spire on the cell-phone device. The device had been locked away at GLENCOM for safe-keeping, but Spire had a recording of the message that Lazarus had left for him, the most significant parts he now knew like some sinister nursery rhyme.

When this recording finishes, you will see a glimpse of the technology, the power I am talking about. This was indeed derived from recovered and reverse-engineered alien artefacts, as incredible as that may seem...

I have hidden the definitive proof you need in order to reveal to the world, what has been happening. You must do this for the greater good of humanity. You will find schematics, a miniature working zero-point energy device, and proof – in the form of a large quantity of Element 115, not found on Earth – of the power source for the gravity-drives used by the E.T craft. The coordinates are already known by you Robert; think hard...your creators, your humble abode!

The revelations in the message were nothing short of incredible. Spire had been racking his brains all week, trying to decipher the last section – *The coordinates are already known by you Robert; think hard...your creators, your humble abode!* How could he know where Lazarus had hidden the things he'd talked about. *Had Lazarus deliberately chosen a location that Spire already knew about? How could that even be possible?*

Spire suddenly slipped on a loose section of path and nearly fell over. He composed himself, checked behind him, and continued up through the dull, grey, misty gloom that surrounded him, accompanied by just the whistling gale that continued to batter the mountain. The two men who had overtaken him were now just grey shadows, fading into the mist up ahead. He'd been walking for forty minutes now, which meant the summit, thankfully, shouldn't be much further.

Spire's thoughts drifted back to the UFO phenomenon and the minefield of truths, half-truths, and lies that it seemed to be. On the one hand, the science was undeniable - 3 million earth like planets, meant that it was inconceivable that ET intelligent life didn't exist elsewhere; but if UFO's were indeed alien visitors, why wasn't there more definite proof. *Why hadn't the aliens made themselves known?* For the first time in history however, the Pentagon had confirmed that the three recently released videos from the gun-cameras of F18 jet fighter jets did indeed depict objects of unknown origin, which displayed anti-gravity, current known laws of physics-defying characteristics. Was this evidence of alien visitation however? Or, merely secret, very advanced, U.S or foreign technology? Spire had no idea, but both options appeared possible.

He continued up, the path becoming more inclined as he neared the summit. Another ten minutes passed and the intermittent gusts of wind became stronger, but the rain thankfully lighter.

Spire negotiated a treacherous part of the path, which now ascended up a carved out stone stairway up along a steep scarp which led to the top of the first peak, thankfully he was nearing the summit.

Visibility was still only limited to about thirty foot in any direction, and without the path it would be easy for anyone to wander off the side of the mountain.

The walk was doing him good though. He still had no answers for what had transpired last week, but at least he felt he'd blown some cobwebs away and he was now more determined than ever to try and solve the puzzle left for him by Professor Lazarus.

Spire made it to the top of the first peak, which was desolate, misty and deserted, and he continued along the flat ridge which connected to the 'proper' summit. Visibility was improving slightly but the wind was buffeting him from all sides. Despite this, from the misty gloom came four men dressed head to toe in black, jogging slowly, no doubt owing to the conditions. The four tough-looking, chisel-jawed men passed him, one of them nodding his head in a show of respect perhaps for Spire's effort in being up there with them on such a horrendous day. They were SAS, no doubt, Spire concluded, heading back down in some kind of timed trial.

Finally Spire reached the plateau of the summit and he made his way over to the 886 m-marked well-preserved, Bronze Age cairn. There were a few people up there, including the two guys who'd passed him, one of them looking quite comical as he grappled with two flags, one in each hand, which he'd now unfurled and were furiously flapping in the gale. His mate was trying to take a picture, no doubt for the next edition of their *Extinction Rebellion* brochure, Spire surmised.

Spire drew is some deep breaths, filling his lungs with cold air as he took in the view, the mist having now cleared somewhat, at least on one side of the mountain anyway.

Spire considered the next twenty-four hours. He'd travel back home to Oakdale tonight and spend the day tomorrow planning his next steps in this, the latest task given to him by GLENCOM. The first thing he needed to do would be to contact Travis Dexter. He'd need his help for sure and Travis lived in Nevada, which was after all, home to Area 51, where Lazarus allegedly worked. Travis had accompanied him on most of his dangerous tasks and had saved his life many times and he had a feeling he'd be depending upon him again in the not too distant future. He'd also need to call Isobel; she'd no doubt be able to provide some much valued expertise with her knowledge of astrobiology and physics, provided he could trust her of course. He still hadn't worked that one out.

With a feeling of renewed energy and intrigue about the forthcoming mission; an investigation of what had to be one of humanities greatest mysteries - *Are we alone? Are we being visited by extra-terrestrial entities?* Spire turned, and started the hour long trek back down the mountain.

CHAPTER 2

Las Vegas, Nevada

TRAVIS DEXTER SHIFTED restlessly on his chair. He'd been seated at the same Blackjack table in the Sahara Casino Hotel, on Las Vegas Blvd, for the last three hours. In between playing cards and admiring the female croupier's breasts – the fourth to deal since he'd been there, and by far the most attractive, he'd been knocking back Whiskey Sours, his favourite drink and for a change winning money, and plenty of it. He estimated he must have had at least ten shots, and was now up around twenty-thousand dollars, give or take.

He was starting to feel a little light-headed, but wasn't sure if it was the attractive croupier making him feel like that, or the alcohol. He smiled at her as she paused for him to bet. He then pushed a stack of one hundred dollar chips into the betting-box on the green felt table and took another sip of his drink, glancing up at the attractive redhead as she started to deal.

"Place your bets please, gentlemen," she said, whilst continuing to look at Dexter.

An elderly man had just taken a seat next to Dexter and he pushed a ten-dollar chip into the box in front of him He nodded at him, while adjusting his Stetson.

"Feeling lucky, cowboy?" Dexter asked, raising his eyebrows.

"I've been having plenty of luck today, but it's all bad."

"I know that feeling!" Dexter replied, as the croupier slid a card over to each of them, face up, and dealt herself a Five of Clubs. She then dealt a second card to each of them. Dexter looked down at the Queen of Spades and Nine of Diamonds face up on the green table in front of him.

The old cowboy's cards totalled fifteen.

"Sir?" the croupier asked the old man.

"Ah, a card, p..."

Dexter cut him off. "Stick on that cowboy. The dealer has a five."

Dexter stayed with nineteen. The croupier then pulled a Ten of Hearts. She pulled a third card, another six. "Twenty-two," she said. "See, your luck is changing already," she said, smiling.

The old cowboy nodded at Dexter, and offered him his hand. "Gregson, Neil Gregson is the name. And thanks, I'll remember that tip for the future."

Dexter shook his hand. "No problem buddy," I'm Travis Dexter.

"Bets please, gentlemen," the attractive croupier said, interrupting them.

Dexter doubled up on his last bet, leaving two-thousand dollars in the betting box, prompting one of the casino's pit-bosses to stroll over from another table. The official glanced at stack of chips, appeared to make a mental calculation of the amount in the betting box, before nodding at the croupier and wandering away again.

The croupier dealt Dexter a four and a seven, against her Ten of Clubs. The old cowboy had a pair of Jacks and stayed.

"Card," Dexter said, downing the last of his whiskey sour.

From the pack, the croupier dealt him a King of Spades. "Twenty-one!" she said, pulling a card for herself. She turned it over to reveal Nine of Diamonds. "You both win," she said, flashing a smile. The pit boss stood in silence as the croupier counted out three-thousand dollars and paid Dexter.

"Nice one, Travis," Gregson said, tipping his hat.

"Thank you very much, Amber," Dexter said, pushing a hundred dollar chip over to her.

"Why, thank you, Mr," she said, with a lingering smile.

The pit boss nodded nonchalantly as Dexter manoeuvred his six foot-two-inch frame from his seat, and stood up. "See you around, old timer," he winked at Gregson, and thank *you* Amber, he said, before making his way over to *Carlito's Bar* situated at the rear of the casino, for a final drink.

He took a seat and ordered another Whiskey Sour and a minute later the bartender placed the drink down on the bar in front of him.

As he sat there, he pondered over the last big private job he'd done, helping his good friend, Robert Spire and the U.K's GLENCOM prevent a gang of thugs and ex-military drop outs from unwittingly releasing a deadly alien virus that had arrived on Earth on a meteorite. Never in his wildest dreams had he considered he'd be involved in such a thing. It had seemed so far-fetched, that was until Covid-19 had come along. The emergence of some sinister virus from bats in China had reminded him that nothing could be taken for granted. It was scary stuff. Dexter had discharged himself from the US Army some years ago. He'd drawn the line with Afghanistan, Gulf War's one and two had been enough for him. The U.S. Government weren't going to send him on any more wild goose chases around more dusty hell-holes, that much was certain. As he reached for his drink, a musky, pleasant scent wafted into his nostrils.

"You going to get me one of those, baby?" the leggy croupier, from earlier asked, taking a seat on the bar stool next to him. "I just got off, so figured I'd come and say hi."

"Sure, what would you like?"

"A gin and tonic, with plenty of fruit would be great," she said, smiling.

The bartender nodded, made up her drink and placed it on the bar, together with a small tray of nuts.

"Here's to a lucky night," she said, raising her glass toward Dexter. "So you're Travis right?" she asked, placing the drink back down on the bar.

"Sure am," Dexter said.

"Well, Travis, I just wondered if you fancied spending some of your hard won money on me tonight."

Dexter allowed his eyes to wander over Amber's athletic but curved body, very visible through her clinging black dress.

"Well, do you like what you see?"

Dexter slugged his drink. "What do you have in mind?"

She looked at him seductively. "Well maybe a late lunch, or early dinner and then, well we can see?" she said, crossing her legs slowly.

"It's a deal," Dexter said, paying the barman for the drinks and tipping him handsomely. They both headed out of the main casino area passing the numerous gaming tables and slot machines, all of which were emitting annoying, electronic melodies, and headed over to the bank of elevators in the main corridor. "I know a nice discreet Italian restaurant one block from here," Dexter said, as he nodded to a security guard standing by the elevator.

The pair of them headed down to the main foyer and out into the midday sun.

Following linguine pasta and Pacific shrimp lunch, and a decent bottle of Chianti, they both headed back to the Sahara where Dexter had booked a room for a fortnight, as he usually did when on a gambling binge. He much preferred being able to roll up into bed at whatever time it suited him.

They headed up to the seventeenth floor and back to his hotel room. "Make yourself at home," he said, closing and locking the door behind him.

"Very nice suit," Amber said. "If I stay here, at least I'll be early for my next shift," she said, raising her eyebrows at him.

"Well I won't be kicking you out until at least eight a.m.," Dexter replied, half-joking as he headed into the bedroom and over to the wardrobe, where he slid the door back and opened up the combination-lock safe inside. Inside was his guardian angel; a Desert Eagle semi-automatic pistol. He removed the Israeli manufactured personal cannon, checked it was loaded and slid it under the bed, out of sight. He wasn't expecting any trouble, but he never took any chances, especially with women who appeared too good to be true.

He closed and locked the safe back up, slid the wardrobe closed and headed back into the lounge area of the suite. Can I get you a drink?" he asked, walking back in, a familiar musky scent filling the room.

"A gin and tonic, or Champagne, if you have some, would be great," she said. "Do you mind if I take a shower? I usually have one as soon as I get in from work."

"Yeah sure, make yourself at home," Dexter said, heading over to the mini bar to get the drinks. As he did, he glanced at himself in the full length mirror and lifted his shirt up. He tensed his powerful trunk, his pectoral and abdominal muscles rippled in response. Years of military training had kept him in great physical condition, despite his advancing age. He didn't quite know how he'd reached 52, but he had. He ruffled up his still dark brown, but greying on the sides' hair, pulled open the fridge and grabbed a bottle of Crystal Champagne.

Amber walked back in wearing nothing but a white cotton bathrobe, black G-string visible underneath. Dexter corked and poured two glassed of champagne and handed a glass to her, before kissing her on her neck. The scent of her perfume and the alcohol he'd consumed combined into an intoxicating pleasurable mix.

"Bottoms up," she said.

"My favourite position," Dexter replied.

They both sipped their drinks, and then Dexter took her glass and placed it on the table by the side of the coffee-coloured leather sofa, before pushing her back onto it.

"Hey, take it easy cowboy," she said to him, giggling.

Dexter knelt on the floor between her open legs and kissed Amber's navel, before moving down towards her black panties. He kissed her and started to pull off her G string with his teeth, Amber squeezing her soft thighs against his rough jaw in response.

Just as he was about to pleasure her, Dexter's smartphone rang. Normally he'd have ignored it, but it was a unique ring tone which he'd not heard in a good while and it belonged to his good friend, Robert Spire.

Dexter got up. "Sorry honey but I need to take this call," he said.

"No! Don't stop now, please," Amber groaned.

Dexter ignored her, grabbed his phone from the side table and answered it. "Well if it isn't my globe-trotting, trouble-seeking good buddy from the U.K.," he said, affectionately.

"Hey, well that's a greeting and a half. How you doing Travis? I hope I'm not interrupting a card game or anything equally important this afternoon?"

"A little of both, but don't worry about it," Dexter said, taking a gulp of champagne. So what do I owe the pleasure of this call for then Robert?"

There was a short silence on the end of the phone.

"Well, something has come up. Something very important and it looks like I'll need your help," Spire said.

"Now you do have my full attention," Dexter said, winking at Amber to show her he'd not forgotten her.

"Did you hear the news about the American Professor, Robert Lazarus?"

"I sure did, saw it on CNN yesterday. He was the guy who reckoned he worked on crashed saucers for the U.S. Government over at Area 51, right?"

"That's the chap yep. He was about to release some information, a paradigm-changing secret technology, but was assassinated before he had the chance. It's a long story and I won't go into it on the phone but it turns out he left a posthumous message for me to continue his quest."

"What a surprise. I've no idea how you get yourself tied up in these things, but I'm glad you do, it keeps me busy."

"Very funny, but I'm glad you're always willing to help Travis. I couldn't do some of these missions without you, you know that."

"Well of course I am buddy, especially if Her Majesty's Government will be assisting with expenses."

"I've no doubt they will," Spire replied.

"Well count me in. I assume you'll want to meet soon?" Dexter asked.

"Yep, that's a given. Lazarus was based in Nevada, so it seems like the appropriate place to start," Spire confirmed.

"Well I'll be ready and waiting for your call, Robert."

"Great, I need some sleep. I'll let you get back to whatever you were doing," Spire said.

"Very kind of you. I'll fill you in on that later," Dexter said, ending the call.

"Couldn't that have waited?" Amber asked, looking a bit moody as she finished her Champagne.

"No it couldn't have, but now you have my full attention again," Dexter said, refilling her glass.

"Well you'd better be ready to fuck me now, cowboy," she whispered.

"That's an invitation I can't refuse," Dexter said as he moved on top of Amber and slowly penetrated her.

Amber groaned with pleasure. "Oh babe, that's more like it," she whispered.

Dexter sighed. Amber felt good, but his mind was already wandering to the intriguing mission that lay ahead and to seeing his old buddy, Robert Spire once again.

CHAPTER 3

Oakdale, Wales

SPIRE ROLLED OUT of bed and lay on his back, stretching for five minutes as he readied his body for some morning exercise. He felt a little relieved following the call with Travis before he'd gone to sleep, knowing he'd be available to help him on this latest mission. Spire turned over and did his usual one-hundred sit ups, followed by sixty push-ups.

He stretched again, before heading into the kitchen to make a pot of fresh coffee. As he waited for the coffee to brew, he turned the T.V. on and flicked it over to Sky News. Lingering Brexit issues were still in the news, but at least the Covid-19 situation was more under control now that the vaccine had been rolled out. Who could have guessed that the U.K. would have teamed up with Russian scientists to combine the *Oxford* and *Sputnik V* vaccines to produce an even more highly effective antidote? It was great to see the two nations working together again for something positive.

Spire made some toast with butter and marmalade to go with his coffee, and after finishing breakfast took a quick shower. It was Friday and he needed to go to the office, check on Kim and make sure everything was running smoothly there.

He left and locked up the cottage and drove into town and pulled into the rear car park belonging to his law office, and parked up. He entered via the back door, noting the alarm had been deactivated. He could hear Kim typing away as he headed upstairs.

"Hey, morning, stranger, welcome back," Kim said, looking up from her computer screen as he walked in.

"Do I know you?" Spire said, smiling.

"Ha-ha, very funny. You should do, I'm the person that does all your work for you and feeds your pets!"

Spire raised his arms up in submission. "Fair point, I'm not going to argue with you on that. I'm eternally grateful," he said.

"Can I get you a mug of fresh coffee? I need one," Kim asked, getting up from her desk.

"Never say no to a coffee," Spire replied, entering his office and sitting down at his desk. He stared at the pile of letters in front of him, before swivelling his chair to face the wall-mounted plasma TV, turning it on to BBC World News. There was another march, this time in Paris, the placards in the marchers hands read;

UFO's: Divulgation Maintenant

Spire watched with interest as the group of one-hundred or so marchers walked up towards the *Champs Elysees*. A blond female news reporter was standing on the street, speaking into a microphone, the crowd walking in front and around her.

She spoke in French, the translated text scrolling across the screen. "We are witnessing an extraordinary scene here in Paris, this morning. A growing number of people are demanding that the government disclose all they know about extra-terrestrials and UFO's following the assassination of renowned physicist Professor Robert Lazarus a few weeks ago. This growing movement follows on from similar marches in London and other parts of the world, after people it seems have become convinced that we are indeed being visited from entities from other worlds, and that our governments do indeed know a lot more than they are letting on. This is Emilee Trimaud reporting."

Spire shook his head in amazement, and turned back to his desk. His mind really wasn't focussed on the law, but he needed to check through the incoming mail.

Kim walked in with two cups of coffee and sat down in front of him. "So what's going on this time?" she asked.

"Have you seen the news?"

Kim looked passed Spire at the screen, raising her eyebrows at what she saw. "Good Lord, UFO's, are you serious?"

"I'm afraid so. That's what GLENCOM have asked me to look into following the slaying of that American professor the other week."

"You're kidding me right. They've asked you to hunt for little green men?! I thought they were a serious organisation, Rob. What are they going to do, send you to Mars?!" Kim said, laughing.

"Don't you believe in extra-terrestrial life?"

Kim sipped her coffee. "It's not really something I've thought too much about if I'm honest. There are enough problems and things to think about on this planet to be considering whether there's life elsewhere. Anyway it's a very scary thought."

Spire flicked the TV off and looked at Kim. "I've been doing some research, and I know it's a very controversial subject but the more you know about the topic, the harder it is to deny there's something very real about it."

"Well, I know very little about it and I'm not sure I even want to know!"

Spire tutted. "You need to have an open mind at least. Did you know that there was a series of sightings, a UFO flap as they're called, down here in West Wales in the late 1970's?"

Kim looked at Spire; her pretty eyes widening as he spoke. "Are you trying to scare me now?"

"Not at all."

"So you're being serious?"

"Well yes. Take a look at this," Spire said, turning his chair to face the T.V. He grabbed the control and navigated onto the internet and searched for *Welsh Triangle UFO*, turning the LED screen so that Kim could take a closer look.

"Back in 1977 there was a series of sightings around here, dubbed the Welsh Triangle as most of the sightings seemed to be grouped around Little Haven, RAF Brawdy as it then was, and a farm on the headland."

"And what was being seen?" Kim asked, now intrigued.

"Well, the occupiers of the farm had multiple experiences, from a number of cattle vanishing from the milking sheds and appearing in a field some way away, the family car being chased by orbs of light to seeing a figure wearing what was described as a typical space suit staring through the farm window, which caused the T.V. to go nuts with static."

Kim giggled. "Are you being serious, spacemen down in Little Haven?!"

"Not only that, but many villagers saw lights in the sky, and the owners of a local hotel there even apparently saw a silver disc land in their back field, and occupants, again in space suits, seemingly measuring or inspecting the ground there. Turns out that there was a nuclear underground bunker there which some have suggested they were interested in."

"That's nuts!" Kim said, finishing her coffee.

"I'm not convinced we were being visited by aliens back then, but something very weird was going on. Don't forget, it was at the height of the cold war, RAF Brawdy was an active U.S. base, which it turns out was being used to listen to and track Russian submarines out in the Atlantic."

"Wow! Really? I never knew things were that exciting down here in the 1970's," Kim joked.

"I mean just one of those events could easily be brushed off, drunk farmers maybe. But, when you have the farm sightings, the hotel, other locals seeing things, and these school kids," Spire said, finding the page he was looking for on the smart T.V., "then you do have to wonder what the hell was going on."

Kim and Spire watched the old _BBC news clip_ in silence.

The article described how fourteen pupils from the _Broad Haven Primary School_ said they'd spotted a UFO in a field near their playground, with the children separately describing seeing a silver _cigar-shaped_ craft, with a _dome covering the middle third,_ land in a field behind the school, where there happened to be a water treatment works.

Some of the children had even drawn what they said they'd seen, and an image of one of the drawings popped up on the screen.

"Well, I have to admit, that does look like a flying saucer, not a tractor," Kim said, now intrigued. "Look one of them has even drawn a cute little alien," she added.

Spire sighed. "That's the problem; it's hard for people to take this stuff seriously when they look at pictures like this, but I'm convinced the children drew what they'd actually seen."

The news clip finished and Spire flicked the T.V. off and turned back to Kim.

"Wow, its mega interesting though I agree. Has anything happened down here since?" Kim asked.

Spire shook his head. "Not to my knowledge. It's all very odd. Seems to have been a concentration of intense happenings for a few years, not just a few days / nights, but nothing as far as I'm aware since in or around 1979."

"It's just weird. It does sound like the military could be involved though, don't you think?"

"It's highly possible. The interesting thing is that with the recent release of the MOD's UFO files by the British Government, documents came to light confirming that the MoD's UFO project asked the RAF Police to conduct a secret investigation into these mysterious events, while Parliament, the media and the public were being told the subject was of no defence significance. It was even suggested that what the kids saw must have been an RAF Harrier Jump Jet on a training exercise."

"Well, can't those planes hover?" Kim asked.

"Yeah, but while making a horrendous roar, scaring the living daylights out of anyone nearby, not to mention blowing debris far and wide."

"That's true," Kim said. "I was lucky enough to be very close to a coastguard helicopter taking off, up in Snowdonia. It was amazing, but yeah, very noisy and it blasted leaves and anything else that was on the ground away as it took off."

"Exactly, there's no way these kids mistook the craft for a Harrier, just doesn't add up. They describe seeing a cigar-shaped object moving silently beyond the trees. Just look at the drawings, I mean come on."

Kim shook her head in agreement with Spire's comment, and was silent for a moment before her eyes lit up. "Why don't you and I go and see if we can find the farm and the hotel down in Little Haven and take a look. It's not that far away."

Spire sat there for a moment, studying the pile of post on his desk. "Mm, that's not a bad idea. I did think about doing that after I read about it in *The Welsh Triangle*, but never bothered." Spire looked at his watch. "It's coming up for ten now. Shall we try and get down there for around two? I can trawl through some of this work and we can go if you fancy. We'll be there in forty minutes."

Kim looked at him and smiled. "Great, I'm actually looking forward to this. It's just so intriguing," she said, high-fiving him.

"So what do we have here then," Spire asked, referring to the work, as Kim stood up.

"Not a lot, Rob. The Howard case is going pear-shaped. Client is refusing to accept the most recent offer of forty grand. We've exhausted all medical expert opinion options and the barrister's latest advice is that she must take the money, or she'll be at risk on costs."

"Hmm, okay I'll take a look at it urgently. If she doesn't accept there's not much more we can do apart from come off the court record. Her legal expense insurance won't continue to back this if the offer is a good one."

"The airport fumes case settled on Friday; twenty thousand pounds. And, we have received two new claims this morning. All personal injury, nothing complicated. I'll open the files, get the standard letters done and leave them on your desk for you to deal with, when you get the chance!"

"Good, well done. Nice settlement on the airport case, it was a tricky one."

Spire started sifting through his post. "I guess I'd better respond to this pile of felled trees. Anything I don't finish I'll leave on my desk for you to deal with," he said, giving Kim a wink.

Kim rolled her eyes. "Yes, boss. I'll finish what I'm doing and then we can head down to Little Haven."

"Sounds good. I'll give you a shout at one," Spire said.

CHAPTER 4

SENTENZA HAD PULLED into a service station for a break following his long drive down from London to Wales. He'd had his mission extended by *Quell Tech* in order to try and secure and recover Lazarus' device from the Englishman, Spire, or whoever else might have it. Spire was the most obvious candidate. He either had it, or knew who did, he was sure of that.

He ordered a double expresso and took it over to a secluded table in the corner of the café and sat down. Sentenza had been researching the area of Wales where Spire lived and had quickly made a curious connection, with the UFO sightings that had taken place down here during the late 1970's. Sentenza made sure nobody was paying any abnormal attention to him, and pulled out an A4 file from his leather hold-all that he'd been sent by his contact back in the U.S., marked, *UFOs - Wales, U.K. Unexplained Cases.*

Sentenza had of course been briefed on the Welsh cases some years earlier, but had never researched them in any detail, assuming that most had a rational explanation, but he kept an open mind that some of the sightings may well have been genuine. Most, if not all of them had to have been simply miss-sightings or embellished stories. He settled into his chair and started thumbing through the voluminous file.

The first thing he found was a newspaper clipping from a 1977 edition of the *Carmarthenshire Herald,* about a sighting by a Mrs Louise Barnett and her husband, both aged thirty-one. The couple ran a steak restaurant in Carmarthen and lived in a home set in six wooded acres near the coast. Their credibility seemed unquestionable and they didn't strike

Sentenza as the sort of people who'd be making up UFO stories.

He continued reading whilst sipping his coffee, Mrs Barnett confirming that it was a 10-mile journey from their Carmarthen restaurant to their home and that she had been driving back in the early hours one morning through the dark Welsh countryside. The air was heavy, a storm having just rolled in from the Atlantic and low-lying cloud obscured the normally millions of visible stars. The witness claims that in some far off fields she saw a brown mass, with flat blue lights intermittently flashing. She naturally assumed that there had been an accident farther up the road, but as she got closer, she was surprised to observe that the object looked as if it was hovering in the air, not a police car on the road as she'd expected. Her car radio then went on the blink, just white noise and static. Mrs Barnett travelled on towards Towy Castle, then, whilst continuing to observe, the lights moved towards Trimsaran.

When I reached the spot where I thought it had been, there was nothing. I've never seen anything like it before. I've got perfect vision and I was totally sober. I've never believed in flying saucers before.

Mrs Barnett, completely mystified by her experience, made some inquiries but could find no rational explanation. The police had confirmed that no police cars, fire engines or ambulances had been anywhere near that location and neither the RAF nor private helicopters had been operating.

It turned out that the radio interference had also been widespread, with people all over the area making complaints to radio dealers and the BBC about signal strength. It had fallen off so badly that colour sets had even reverted to black and white.

Sentenza read the account with interest. There was nothing that indicated the sighting had been truly extra-terrestrial, more likely military, he considered.

He continued to the next report, which told of another sighting in almost exactly the same location, but one month later, where more Carmarthenshire residents witnessed a similar happening, again in the early hours. A Mr John Motts, a prominent Welsh artist, was at his home, which enjoys a magnificent view across the estuary. The time was just after 1.00 a.m. and he was preparing for bed after having worked late. He had just switched off the lights in the living room and was drawing back the curtains. Whilst doing so he looked south eastwards across the estuary above and beyond the horizon of hills overlooking Ferryside on the far side of the river, when his eye was suddenly caught by a horizontal strip of light; a luminous pale gold, like the colour of the moon. He thought it must have been part of the moon showing through a gap in the clouds, but it became obvious that the outline shape of light was clear and sharp, far from woolly-edged as it would be from a cloud. Wondering whether the object would move up or down, left or right, the witness was surprised to see the light suddenly blink out, just like turning off a light.

A neighbour of Mr Motts also saw the phenomenon, as did a few other local residents. One female witness described walking from her sitting room, looking through the window and stopping in her tracks, as she saw, just above the level of the land, an extraordinary bright light where there was no reason for a light to be.

The reports went on and on, dozens of them, from simple, honest Welsh folk who had no interest in drawing attention to themselves down here in one of the most rural settings of any place in the world, Sentenza considered.

Sentenza finished his coffee, slid the reports back into the folder and packed it away into his bag. Something seemed to have occurred down here all those years ago, just quite what, he didn't know. The fact that Spire also lived down here seemed to just be a coincidence. He stood up, headed for the restroom and then left the services, checking he wasn't being tailed by anyone as he pulled back onto the M4 Motorway for the remainder of his journey to Pembrokeshire.

CHAPTER 5

Broad Haven
Pembrokeshire

SPIRE ACCELERATED DOWN the quiet, duel carriageway, the Range Rover swallowing up the miles, the wind turbines on the mountain in the distance glinting in the dying afternoon sun, now poking through the clouds.

Twenty minutes later, Spire and Kim drove into Haverfordwest, a quaint, bustling little market town set high on a hill and overlooking a picturesque river and an old castle. They continued through the town following a signpost to the village of Broad Haven, which took them on a country road through undulating and windswept Atlantic coastal countryside. Short trees and hedgerows leaned at unruly angles, but mainly at forty-five degrees, bent over by the Atlantic westerly wind.

They continued on, passing stone farmhouses nestled at the end of long lanes and endless fields of sheep and cattle. Spire slowed down as a tractor pulled out from a lane up ahead. The driver pulled over, allowing him just enough room to slip passed it. Spire rounded a bend and then drove over the crest of a hill and down a steep narrow road which descended towards a curving sandy beach and the normally blue waters of St Brides Bay, which now looked as grey and foreboding as the Atlantic Ocean beyond.

"I think Little Haven is the next bay along," Kim said, surveying the view.

"I think you're right," Spire replied, continuing along the route until the road ascended again through some high, grass-banked lanes before dropping down towards the quiet, fishing village of Little Haven. The village was situated around a very small harbour; fishing boats and dinghy's bobbed up and down in the afternoon swell, the harbour itself overlooked by numerous guest houses up on the rocky cliffs and dotted around the pretty harbour.

"So, where are we going exactly?" Kim asked.

"Well, the Haven Forte Hotel, the site of the alleged UFO landing is around here somewhere, but I thought it was on higher ground," Spire said, slowing down to let an elderly couple cross the road. He slid down his window as the couple stepped onto the pavement. "Excuse me, do you know where the Haven Forte Hotel is?" he asked.

The man looked a little confused, but then his wife said something to him.

"Oh, I think you might mean the old hotel up on the ridge, which is for sale. If so, it's back up the road you just came down, but you need to take the first right as you're going up the hill," the elderly man said, pausing to cough into a handkerchief.

Spire thanked him and slowly pulled off, turning around in a car park that served the small harbour, before driving back up the steep hill they'd just come down, this time taking a sharp right which he'd not seen on the way in. An old, weathered, wooden sign, partly damaged read;

Haven Forte Hotel – Cream Teas Available.

"Oh, I could do with a scone right now," Kim said.

"I think we'll be lucky. I'm sure the hotel has been up for sale for a while, I checked online."

They continued up the narrow lane, and then saw the Haven Forte Hotel hidden off the road, perched high on some rough ground, looking like it hadn't seen a lick of paint for a long time.

Spire pulled the Range Rover off the lane and up the short, overgrown driveway and killed the engine. "No wonder this place hasn't sold. It's clearly seen better days."

"You can say that again. I don't think we'll be getting a cream tea in there," Kim said, frowning.

"We can get you one of those in the village later, don't worry. Come on, let's get out and have a look around."

Spire and Kim got out of the car and headed over towards the front of the building, which looked as if the owners had vacated a good while ago. Spire walked up to a white, brick extension eye-sore, which clearly wasn't part of the original old building and looked through the window. "This looks like your tea room," he said, observing some old tables with chairs stacked upside down on top of them, watched over by two full standing suits of armour placed up against the far wall. It looked like a storeroom full of old props.

"Spooky," Kim said, looking through the windows.

"Come on, let's check around the side of the building," Spire said.

They walked around the left side of the hotel and Spire cupped his hands against the old, lead windows and looked through the glass. As his eyes adjusted to the internal light, he suddenly reeled back in surprise. Inside the room was a woman wearing a thick jumper, laptop on her knees and holding a mug of tea or coffee.

"Jeez, there's someone in there!" he exclaimed.

"Really? Come on, I think we should go," Kim said, sounding a little freaked out.

"Yeah, let's go...to the front door."

"What for?" Kim asked.

"Um, to ring the doorbell!" Spire smiled.

"Ask a silly question," Kim said, rolling her eyes.

They both headed around to the front of the building and Spire pressed the doorbell, which was half hanging out of its fixing on a frame next to the old wooden, castle-like door.

"Did that even ring?" Kim asked, looking nervous.

"Not sure, we'll soon find out," Spire said, looking through the small arched window pane set into the door.

A full minute later, and just as Spire was about to give up, a shadowy figure appeared behind the door, followed by the sound of a key rattling in the door and deadbolts being pulled back.

The door creaked open. "Can I help you?" an Italian-looking lady, in her 70's, asked.

Spire glanced at Kim, then back to the lady at the door. "Um, yes, sorry to disturb you, but we live down here and happened to be passing. I'm doing a bit of research into the events that took place down here in the late 1970's, and hoped you'd be able to give us five minutes of your time," he said.

"You mean the UFO stuff?" the woman said, matter-of-factly.

"Err, yes; I understand you some strange things around here, including something land in your front garden?" Spire asked, feeling a little silly.

"Actually it was my mother; I was only in my early twenties at the time, hard to believe now I know," she said, smiling. "My mother saw it from the rear top floor hall window. It landed in the fields out the back," she said.

"Wow, really? Can you recall what she saw?"

The lady smiled. "Well, like I said, it's a long time ago now, and I was in Spain at the time, but she told me the story hundreds of times. It was late and she'd been cleaning up the restaurant and getting things ready for the next day. As she was on her way to bed, she heard a kind of humming noise coming from outside and noticed an intense bright light coming through the window at the end of the corridor. She went to the window to look out, and in the rear field, saw what she described as an oval-shaped craft, with two humanoid figures dressed in silver suits, walking around in the field, looking as if they were taking measurements of the ground. My mum was a no-nonsense sort of woman. She was not the type of person who would make stuff up, or believe in aliens."

Spire was taken aback by the woman's frankness. "That's incredible. Do you have a lot of land back there?" is all he could say.

"It's a couple of acres, feel free to go back there and take a look. You'll have to be careful though. We placed two caravans and an old boat in the access lane, stop campers and intruders getting in there."

"That's very kind of you. So how long did the event last?" Spire asked, becoming intrigued with the woman's frankness.

"I think about five minutes. We had all sorts of people calling here back then. People even came down from London to ask questions."

"You mean government people?"

"Yes, I believe so."

Spire looked at Kim, who was also now engrossed in what the owner was telling them.

"Can I ask if you know anything about a nuclear bunker being on or near your land?"

The woman looked confused and then said; "That's odd you should say that. A man did come down from London a few years back and said he'd bought a nuclear bunker from an online auction; he asked me where it was. I had to tell him I didn't know."

34

"That's very odd," Spire said, going on to explain that he'd read a book about the events, and that there was supposed to be a nuclear bunker around here somewhere and that was what the UFO, or whatever it was might have been interested in.

The lady shrugged. "I have no idea. All I know is that lots of odd things were going on back then, around here, over at the farm on the headland and out over in the bay around Stack Rocks."

Spire was somewhat lost for words. When someone tells you, very sincerely that an event that happened over forty years ago, did indeed happen, what could he say? If it all been a joke, perhaps made up to attract customers for example, then surely she'd have come clean about it after all this time. If the family had made it up to attract visitors, it clearly hadn't worked.

"So is this place for sale?" he asked.

"Yes, for some time now. I'm hoping we've found a buyer. I'm moving back to Spain. I think they plan on building apartments here," she said, looking tired.

Spire glanced at Kim, then back to the owner. "I really appreciate the time you've given us. Will it be okay if we go around the back to have a look?" he asked.

"Sure, feel free. I won't come. Just be careful," she said, before smiling at them both and closing and locking the door.

Spire looked at Kim and shrugged. "Well, let's go see if we can see where the UFO landed," he said, smiling.

CHAPTER 6

SPIRE AND KIM headed back around the right side of the property and over to where an old caravan and boat had been positioned, effectively blocking the route to the rear of the premises.

"Be careful here," Spire said, as he squeezed between the caravan and the thick scrub that lined the narrow opening to the fields beyond.

They both managed to get through and emerged into the field beyond at the rear of the property, which was much larger than Spire had anticipated. It had to be a good three acres or so; certainly big enough for a large otherworldly craft to land in, if that was indeed what had happened.

"This is crazy, I'm not sure what you expect to find back here," Kim said, stumbling over a large tuft of grass.

"I'm not either, but I just want to see what kind of view the owner's mother would have had from the rear window back in 1977. And if we can see any signs of a nuclear bunker back here, to substantiate some of the things I read about."

"Well the entrance to a nuclear bunker shouldn't be hard to miss, and you could land the *Millennium Falcon* back here and still have room next to it for a couple of *X-Wings*," Kim joked.

Spire looked at her. "Very funny, but I do love the *Star Wars* analogies."

They continued towards the far corner of the field and scoured the ground for anything that looked like a circular depression, or evidence that something heavy had touched down here, but neither of them could see anything. Perhaps looking down from high above something could be seen, but he doubted it after all this time.

"One thing was certain however, old Rosa, the previous owner would have had a perfect view from the rear, upper floor corridor window of anything landing here," Spire commented, as he and Kim both stood there, looking back at the hotel from the rear of the field.

"Well yes, that's obvious from this vantage point. She'd have had amazing views out across St Brides Bay too," Kim added.

"Sadly we aren't going to be able to find any landing marks," Spire half-joked. "Would be interesting to scan the ground with a Geiger counter or electromagnetic detector, see if anything showed up," he added.

Kim passed her right hand over the top of her head, signalling she had no idea what he was talking about.

Spire ignored her and walked up to the side hedge and looked along it, then headed over to what appeared to be something marked out by wooden stakes in the ground, but instead of finding the entrance to a nuclear bunker, the staked area of land appeared to be marking a drainage gully.

"I can't see anything that looks like a bunker around here, can you?"

Kim shook her head. "Nope. Surely the entrance would need to be fairly obvious, not just an obscure hole in the ground."

"You'd have thought so," Spire said, a little disappointed as he turned to take one last look at the hotel. "Come on, let's get out of here."

CHAPTER 7

SPIRE REVERSED THE Range Rover back off the overgrown driveway, headed back down the hill to the small village of Little Haven, passing the quaint cafes and pubs and then headed back up the steep hill towards the coastal road and onto Rippercorn Farm, where more alleged sightings had taken place 45 or so years ago. After that, they could loop back around and be home for around 7 p.m.

The weather was drawing in, with dark clouds rolling in from the Atlantic and the light beginning to fade. "So, remind me of what supposedly went on at the farm then?" Kim asked, as she glanced out over the coastal road towards the ocean.

Spire slowed to take a sharp corner before answering. "Well the family living there, dairy farmers, Billy and Paula I believe their names are, and their five children, back in 1977 reported repeated close encounters with UFO's. The encounters left a trail of burned out cars and TV sets and even spiralling electricity bills caused by supposed magnetic interference, it seems. On one occasion Paula was driving with her children along the country lane back towards home and was pursued by a fiery object shaped like a rugby football."

"You're kidding," Kim said, holding back a smile.

"Sounds ridiculous I know, but I have read umpteen articles and seen numerous documentaries now which confirm very similar phenomena, glowing orbs of lights etc., witnessed by people from all over the world."

Kim raised her eyebrows.

"Later the couple claimed a herd of their cows were inexplicably teleported from a locked field into an adjacent farmyard, and the scariest thing they described was the appearance of a seven foot tall figure in a spacesuit, whose blank face was seen staring through their sitting room window."

"Jesus that would really freak me out," Kim replied.

"Hard to believe I know, but the police were involved, there were multiple witnesses, like the owner of the hotel back there, and indeed don't forget the school kids who say they saw a cigar-shaped UFO, all of whom have all stuck to their stories to this day."

"That's just nuts," Kim said again, shaking her head. "How do we know that somebody wasn't just taking the piss out of these people, pranksters and the like?"

"Well, there has been someone who came forward, I think from the local oil refinery, who said they'd been involved in the entire thing, apparently dressed in a silver asbestos suit to scare a few of the locals. It does kind of make some sense in view of Star Wars having just come out that year."

"Well that makes more sense than aliens visiting us," Kim said.

"It gets more bizarre. An RAF Squadron Leader from RAF Brawdy, who oversaw pilot training from the base, said the description of the suits worn by the *spacemen* did not match anything used by base personnel. It was also an odd coincidence that the airman's son happened to be one of the youngsters who claimed they saw the UFO land behind the school."

"So weird," Kim said.

"I also read that old Rosa from the hotel actually wrote to her MP, a Nicholas Edwards, who became Welsh Secretary in

Mrs Thatcher's Cabinet, to try and get answers from the Ministry of Defence about what was going on."

"What happened?"

"Within days of the MP's intervention, a Squadron Leader from RAF Brawdy visited the hotel to interview Rosa. According to her account, he told them that absolutely nothing at the air base could account for the UFO she'd seen. Apparently he told her it was best not to talk about what she'd seen so as not to alarm the general public. As a result of Westminster getting involved, the MOD later confirmed that there was no record of any unusual activity in the area."

"It's crazy that Westminster and the MOD even got involved. It does suggest something weird was going on down here."

"Exactly," Spire replied. "I think there were attempts to persuade the witnesses from Broad Haven School to admit they had concocted the story, but the kids – now all in their fifties – have stuck doggedly by their story."

Kim remained silent, and just stared out over the cold-looking Celtic Sea, and beyond, the darkening Atlantic Ocean.

Spire rounded a narrow bend, and then accelerated down a long, sweeping hill as they approached the location of the farm which was close to the coastline, overlooking Stack Rocks.

The lanes narrowed into winding tracks, forcing him to slow down. He crossed a junction and as he did, he noticed a white Ford slowly pull out behind him. The vehicle was moving very slowly however and Spire soon lost it in his rear view mirror.

"The farm should be around here somewhere," he said, as they passed the entrances to several farms dotted around the desolate, small part of Wales.

"You can see how something might have happened out here, without anyone really knowing about it. I mean this place is in the middle of nowhere," Kim added.

"You're not kidding," Spire agreed, as he turned a sharp bend, flanked by high hedges on both sides which opened up into another long stretch of road, with stunning views of the ocean through the trees up ahead.

"There it is!" Kim shouted, pointing to a wooden sign hanging at the end of a lane on the right which said;

Lower Rippercorn Farm.

"Well spotted," Spire replied, as he slowed and turned into the private road, before accelerating down the narrow lane, overhanging with thick trees and foliage on both sides.

"This is pretty spooky actually. Imagine a ball of light chasing you down here," Kim commented.

Spire said nothing as he glanced in his rear view mirror, and noted a white car at the entrance to the lane, which appeared to stop, before moving off again. *Was it the Ford from earlier?*

"Hopefully we won't get stopped. This is a private road after all," Spire said, continuing down and checking the rear view mirror again, but seeing no sign of the white car.

They reached the end of the lane where the farmhouse was situated, with views over the bay beyond. He parked up, and cut the engine. "Well, this is the farm where it all supposedly happened. Come on, let's go and take a look."

They both got out of the Range Rover and walked over to the front of the farmhouse. There didn't seem to be anyone around, so Spire walked up to the front door and rang the doorbell. They both waited for a minute or so but nobody answered, so Spire gave a hard rap on the door with his knuckles. Another minute passed, but there was no sign of anyone.

"Does the same family live here after all these years?" Kim asked, looking a little nervous.

"No, I think they moved out a good while ago, now live in Haverfordwest somewhere. I just wanted to ask the current owners if they'd experienced anything odd, but it looks like we're out of luck. Come on, let' get back in the car, drive a little further in."

Spire took a wide arc in front of the farmhouse and proceeded slowly along a road which ran parallel to the sea and traversed open grazing farm land, with fields on both sides full of cattle and sheep. A quarter of a mile or so to the left, the fields ended abruptly in a cliff, with the Celtic Sea and Atlantic visible beyond.

Further along the road, a white vehicle was parked, a van of some description. It didn't look like the vehicle Spire had seen earlier, but he couldn't tell. He slowed to a crawl and pulled over.

"Maybe we should go back?" Kim suggested.

Before Spire could reply, the white car pulled away slowly in the opposite direction, travelling further along the coastal farm road, towards what looked like large cattle sheds at the very end.

"Incredible view of Stack Rocks over to the left," Kim said, as they proceeded along the farm road.

Spire reached the end of the road, which did indeed end with more farm buildings and what he assumed was a huge modern cattle milking shed.

The white van was parked up outside, a steel entrance door to the large shed was banging open and closed, clattering against its frame in the breeze.

"Whoever was driving that van must also work here I guess," Spire said, turning off the engine and getting out. He and Kim headed over to the building's entrance and Spire shouted inside "Hello - excuse me?"

Apart from some distant animal sounds and some clanking from inside somewhere, his call was met with silence. Spire shouted again, but again, no response.

"That's odd. Come on let's go. This is getting creepy," Kim said.

"Hold on," Spire replied, walking further along and around the side of the cow sheds. His view now was a half-open air, vast cow milking shed, stuffed with bales of hay, and a few cows visible at the far end. "Hello?" Spire shouted again.

Again, silence. The individual from the van was either hiding, or simply couldn't hear him shouting.

Spire shrugged and checked his watch. The time was approaching 3.50 p.m. The secrets of Rippercorn Farm would remain, secret, it seemed. "Come on, let's make a move."

"I'll not argue with that suggestion," Kim said, smiling, as they both walked back to the Range Rover.

They drove back down the long lane to the main road. As they emerged from the lane, Spire noticed another building, just off to the right, on the opposite side of the road, which he'd not noticed before. "Hello, that looks unusual," he said, turning right and then pulling the Range Rover back around and stopping alongside the chain barrier in front of the building.

The building was a fairly small, single-story red brick structure, fronted by a small gravel parking area. Spire pulled up and looked out at the sign which was hanging from the chain.

It read;

The Set House: GCI Station
RAF Ripperston, WW II.

There was a number on the sign, so Spire grabbed his smartphone and called it.

"Hello?" A lady answered, in a thick Welsh accent.

Spire greeted her and mentioned he was parked outside the building he'd taken the number from and told her he was interested in what the purpose of the building was.

"Well, we are now closed for winter, but you're welcome to come back during the summer. We are an art gallery." she replied.

"Oh, I see. And what's the link with the R.A.F?" Spire asked, surprised at the response, but more than intrigued as to why there might be a WW II R.A.F post out here.

"Ah, well, the building once housed the newly developed Chain Home Radar System, which was the code name for the ring of coastal early warning radar stations built by the R.A.F., before and during WW II, to detect and track enemy aircraft. It was one of the first early warning radar networks in the world. R.A.F. Ripperston opened as a mobile G.C.I. (Ground Control Intercept) Radar Station in July 1941, I believe."

"Well, that's very interesting," Spire replied, glancing at Kim.

"We restored the building twenty-odd years ago, and now it houses artwork from local artists. Nothing more sinister than that I'm afraid! Set House Arts it's called. Please check out our website. It gives a full history of the RAF connection," the lady said.

"I'll be sure to do that," Spire replied, thanking her for her time and ending the call. He relayed to Kim what the lady had said. "I wonder if the radar was still working when all this stuff was going on," Kim asked.

"Good point. I doubt it, if it was installed in the 1940's but it's worth checking for sure," Spire said, as the chain around the gravelled parking area creaked in response to a sudden gust of wind.

Spire slid his window back up and accelerated away, the Range Rover's 4.4 Litre V8 engine giving a satisfying low growl as he did.

The narrow coastal roads were deserted as they drove back towards Broadhaven and then on towards Oakdale and home. Spire kept an eye out for the white car he'd seen earlier, and whilst he saw glimpses of white vehicles behind him, none of them appeared to be following him. After an hour's drive, he pulled up outside his office to drop Kim off. "Well thanks for that, all very interesting, even though we saw nothing!" Kim said, smiling.

"What did you expect, a silver disc to descend and suck a cow up from a field in its tractor beam," Spire joked.

"Very bloody funny. I'll speak to you tomorrow," Kim said, closing the door and walking to her car.

Spire headed along the narrow lanes for the short journey home, the evening closing in with heavy dark clouds rolling in from the Atlantic. As he drove, he mulled over the encounter with the owner of the Haven Forte Hotel, and her story about the UFO landing in the rear field and the comment she made about someone looking for the bunker that was supposedly on her land. He'd looked, but had found nothing. *Probably nonsense*, he thought. As he pulled onto his driveway, a thought crossed his mind. As soon as he got inside, he'd carry out a check on *Google Earth*, just to see if he could find anything unusual.

CHAPTER 8

Oakdale, West Wales

SPIRE DEACTIVATED HIS home alarm system and stopped the countdown. As the alarm beeped off, a loud *meow* from Charlie, who sounded as if he was in the lounge, greeted him.

"Hello there puss," Spire said, heading straight over to him and giving him some long strokes.

Charlie purred in contentment as Spire looked around to make sure everything looked as it should inside the cottage, which it did. He got up, closed the blinds and put the heating on. Although spring was approaching, the weather had taken a very cold turn and he considered sparking up the log fire. Charlie would appreciate it, if nothing else.

Spire headed into the kitchen, closed the blinds and grabbed his laptop, before heading back into the lounge and pouring a large, XO Cognac for himself. He sat down next to Charlie and booted up his computer. A myriad of search terms were going through his mind; *where to start?*

"Bunker," he muttered to himself. He clicked onto *Google* and typed in; **Haven Fort Hotel and Nuclear Bunker,** and hit the return key.

Nothing of relevance came up, as expected, however the first article which appeared was a *Wales Online* news article about the construction of a nuclear bunker beneath a Carmarthenshire town. Spire clicked onto it.

'Due to an escalation in the Cold War that saw the U.S. planning to install cruise missile bases in the U.K., Conservative Prime Minister, Margaret Thatcher encouraged

local councils to build nuclear shelters, with a promise of a grant to cover the majority of the cost – rumoured to be around £400,000.

For younger generations, it is difficult to imagine the day in 1986, when around 7,000 people descended on Carmarthen town centre to form a human chain in protest at the bunker's construction.'

Spire shook his head, recalling the period quite well, the fear that everyone had back then at the real worry that nuclear war could be imminent. It was a bloody scary period, and it wasn't that long ago.

He looked through the other search returns but found nothing. He then loaded up *Google Earth* and searched for *Little Haven*, in Wales. The glowing Earth globe graphic span around and zoomed down to the U.K., then Wales. Spire quickly found the small bay in the town and then moved up to the *Haven Forte Hotel.* He searched around with the cursor, zooming in and out around the area where he and Kim had walked earlier in the day. He couldn't immediately see anything unusual and reached for his Cognac and took an appreciative sip. He was about to abandon the search, when all of a sudden he saw an odd pattern in what he thought had just been an intersection between hedgerows in the fields. He zoomed up on the spot, and stared, his drink in hand. "Hello, what's this? Looks like I might have found something Charlie," he muttered, staring at the screen in front of him.

Spire was amazed to see that right smack bang in the middle of the *Google* image was a square structure; hidden from view from the vantage point he'd had earlier in the day at ground level. The Haven Fort Hotel was clearly visible on the far left of the image and the structure was right behind the hedge running along the boundary at the back of the hotel's rear field. *Could this be the entrance to the bunker mentioned? And if so, could whoever or whatever had landed there been interested in measuring or maybe mapping this underground structure?* He'd have to go back and investigate further some time. He had so much more to do however, and the task of trying to visit all alleged UFO sighting locations, would be impossible.

Spire turned his mind to *The Rendlesham Forest Incident* to glean a greater insight into what had happened down there, just before Christmas of 1980. He typed it into the search engine whilst Charlie purred and stretched out on the sofa next to him. The first entry was of course a *Wikipedia* entry, and Spire started reading;

In late December 1980, there was a series of reported sightings of unexplained lights near Rendlesham Forest, Suffolk, England which have become linked with claims of UFO landings. The events occurred just outside RAF Woodbridge, which was used at the time by the United States Air Force (USAF). USAF personnel, including deputy base commander Lieutenant Colonel Charles I. Halt, claimed to see things they described as a UFO sighting.

The occurrence is the most famous of claimed UFO events to have happened in the United Kingdom, ranking among the best-known reported UFO events worldwide. It has been compared to the Roswell UFO incident in the United States and is sometimes referred to as "Britain's Roswell".

The UK Ministry of Defence stated the event posed no threat to national security, and it therefore never was investigated as a security matter. Sceptics have explained the sightings as a misinterpretation of a series of nocturnal lights: a fireball, the Orfordness Lighthouse and bright stars.

Spire considered the possible explanations for the event - bright stars and a lighthouse? "You've got to be kidding," he muttered. *How could a bunch of Air Force men charged with security of an important airbase mistake stars and a lighthouse for strange lights and a possible UFO sighting?* He delved further into the event and searched further.

It seems the events took place over three nights, so it wasn't just a brief sighting or glimpse of some lights in the forest. It seems that a security patrol near the East Gate of RAF Woodbridge saw some odd looking lights descending into the nearby Rendlesham Forest, which separated the twin bases. The servicemen initially thought the lights may have come from a crashed aircraft but, upon entering the forest to investigate further they describe seeing a glowing, triangular object, about the size of a car and displaying coloured lights. As they attempted to approach the object, it appeared to move through the trees, although later, one of the airmen claims to have actually walked up to the object and touched it, which he describes as being made from a black glass-like material, and displaying hieroglyphic type markings or symbols.

Spire recalled what he knew about *The Roswell Incident* all those years earlier and the son of the RAAF Base's Major, who claims he was shown some recovered debris, a section of which he described as looking like an I-beam. The son of the major claims he saw violet-coloured hieroglyphics etched along the length of the material. *An odd coincidence*, Spire thought, as he continued reading.

The events in *Rendlesham* start getting even more bizarre with the involvement of the local police force who attended the scene, but who only noted lights coming from the Orford Ness lighthouse, some miles away on the coast. It appears that the morning of 26th December, some servicemen returned to a small clearing where the alleged craft had supposedly landed and found three small impressions on the ground in a triangular pattern, as well as some burn marks and broken branches on nearby trees. The local police re-attended but considered the impressions could have been made by rabbits! Plaster cast impressions of the indentations were however made, it seems.

"Come on, this is ridiculous," Spire muttered. How could trained U.S. airmen, albeit fairly young at the time, many in

their late teens it appears, mistake a potential UFO landing for the lights from a lighthouse and rabbit scrapings?!

Spire continued reading, the events becoming even more interesting on the third night, 28th December 1980. With a Christmas party underway, it seems that a serviceman burst into the party tent and approached the Deputy Base Commander, telling him that the lights were back – the UFO was back. The DBC, determined to resolve what he considered to be ongoing 'nonsense,' took several servicemen out to investigate the alleged site of the earlier 'landing' and the ongoing lights being observed in the forest and in the sky.

Whilst in the forest, the Deputy Base Commander and the servicemen measured radiation readings at the supposed landing site and again witnessed a strange red light in the forest, which appeared to be moving through the trees, described by the DBC as looking like it was winking. He also describes seeing three star-like lights in the sky, two to the north and one to the south, about 10 degrees above the horizon. He said that the brightest of these hovered for two to three hours and seemed to beam down a stream of light to the ground from time to time.

Astronomers have explained away these star-like lights as bright stars, and UFO debunkers the lights in the forest as coming from the lighthouse. Interestingly the DBC had a taken a hand-held tape recorder out with him on that night and had recorded the event as it unfolded. Spire found a link online to the 17 minute recording and listened to it.

The Deputy Base Commander can be heard discussing the clicks emitted by the Geiger counter with the other service men at the forest landing site. At 12.5 minutes in, one of the men can be heard saying that there are some very strange sounds coming from the farmer's field beyond the tree line, and then they see a light, described as a strange, small red light, at which point the farm animals go quiet.

The DBC can be heard saying – *There's no doubt about it, this is weird. It looks like an eye winking at you.* He continues describing what he's seeing, some kind of phenomena, then two strange objects in the sky. At 17 minutes and 20 seconds in, he is heard saying;

Here he comes from the south; he's coming in toward us now! Now were observing what appears to be a beam coming down to the ground! One object over Woodbridge base, lights beaming down.

Spire patted Charlie again. In the DBC's own words, he thought, *there's no doubt about it*, he and the other servicemen appeared to have witnessed something extraordinary. It seems ridiculous to suggest that highly trained military men, assigned to what was no doubt a nuclear base, could have all been fooled by the lights from a distant lighthouse. The last time Spire checked, lighthouses didn't move around in the sky or beam streams of light down to the ground.

Spire stretched and finished off his Cognac, impressed by the obvious excitement and confusion clearly evident in the men's voices on the recording.

"What do you think Charlie; do you believe in little green men?"

Charlie gave a *meow* in response and began purring loudly. "That sounds like a yes," Spire muttered, closing down his laptop. He'd had enough UFO stories for now. As he did, he heard a noise from the back garden, like a plant pot falling over. Spire looked at Charlie, placed the empty glass of Cognac down, and slowly got off the sofa.

CHAPTER 9

SENTENZA FROZE, CURSING under his breath, which he was now holding, knowing Spire was bound to have heard the planter falling from inside. He'd failed to see the dark plant pot he'd just knocked over close to the garden shed, alongside the cottage. Sentenza had spotted Spire and his female companion down in Little Haven earlier, Spire's white Range Rover sticking out like a sore thumb, and had followed them as they'd checked out the locations of the 1977 UFO sightings. Sentenza had to admit, he was enthralled by this sleepy area of Wales, and being here, gave the events he'd been reading about in the files more gravitas. He looked around, and gathering his usual resources, quickly considered his next move.

Spire turned the light off in the lounge, grabbed the iron fire-poker from beside the fire place and opened the French doors which led out to the rear garden, flashlight in hand. *Had the friendly fox returned?* He'd not seen or heard it for a good while. He panned the light around the back of the garden, checking all the dark corners, but couldn't see anything. The fence looked undisturbed, just a strong breeze blowing through the trees that surrounded his cottage. The wind could have been responsible for the sound, blowing something over he figured. He stepped out, gripping the poker tightly and slowly headed along the back of the cottage towards the side path, which led to the shed and rear garden gate.

He shone the torch into the darkness, but couldn't see anything, the garden gate appeared closed, but he couldn't tell for sure. He walked further along, and then noticed a dark terracotta pot lying on its side, just beyond the shed, that the wind or animal perhaps had knocked over. Spire raised the poker above his head; crept along the front of the shed, which was locked with a padlock and, hesitating by the corner, his heart beginning to race, looked behind, ready to strike whoever might be there with the ironwork.

There was nobody there, just a dark corner. Spire let out a deep breath he'd been holding, bent down and placed the pot back upright, and moved it out of the way. He checked the gate, which was still locked. The tall oak trees along his boundary rustled in the wind, just as the *hoot* from a distant owl could be heard.

Spire turned, sensing something was behind him. "Jeez, Charlie, you scared the hell out of me," Spire said, as his cat brushed up against his leg, before jumping up onto the old BBQ in the corner and then onto the wall by the gate. The cat hesitated, looking towards the shed, gave a brief *meow*, before jumping onto the fence and walked along it, disappearing towards the front of the property.

Spire looked around one more time, before heading back along the side of the cottage. Just as he was about to go back inside, he felt his smart phone buzzing in his pocket, causing him to jump again. *Jeez, all this UFO stuff is getting me on edge*, he thought. He headed back in through the French doors, pulling his phone out as he did.

Isobel's name glowed from the screen. He quickly locked the door, placed the poker back by the fireside, and answered the call.

"Hey Robert, how are you?" came Isobel's Russian accent.

"Hi, I'm good. Nice to hear your voice," Spire replied.

"What you up to? Hopefully I'm not disturbing you," Isobel said, sounding as if she was taking a sip from a drink as she spoke.

"I've probably been spending too much time looking into UFO's. It's all starting to put me on edge," Spire said, going on to tell her he'd just come in from the garden armed with a poker to attack a blown-over plant pot.

Isobel laughed. "Well you can never be too cautious."

"Sounds like you've got a drink in your hand; hold on, I'll pour myself another," Spire replied.

"Very astute of you. Yes, you caught me; I'm drinking a vodka tonic."

Spired poured himself another large Cognac and checked through the front lounge windows, before walking into the kitchen and doing the same, and finally closing the blinds.

"Have you had a productive few days?" Isobel asked.

"Interesting day today," Spire said, going on to tell her about what he'd been up to.

"Hmm, all sounds very romantic, driving around the coastline with your female friend," Isobel said.

"Don't be silly. Kim's my secretary-come office manager," Spire replied, not in the mood to explain further.

"I was joking, of course I know she can't possibly be as sexy as me, Robert," Isobel replied.

Spire laughed. "So what have you been up to?"

"Vell, I have been doing some research on Element 115, and vot I have found really is quite interesting," she said, stopping to take a sip of her vodka.

Spire had spoken to Isobel as soon as he'd left GLENCOM; after Lazarus had mentioned the element in his hologram message, and had asked her if she knew anything about the strange-sounding element.

"And?"

"Vell, Element 115, or Moscovium as it is actually called, is a man-made, super-heavy element that has 115 protons in its nucleus. As with all elements on the periodic table, the element's number corresponds to the number of protons in the nucleus of the element's atom. It basically has 23 more protons than the heaviest element that you can find on Earth, which is uranium. It's extremely rare and can be created one atom at a time in particle accelerators. It only exists for a fraction of a second however before it decays into another element."

"So what's so special about it then?" Spire asked.

"It is special because the element is near the predicted, *island of stability,* meaning it could last long enough to have some real practical applications."

Ah-ha, Spire muttered, although he wasn't certain what Isobel was really talking about.

"Element 115 was discovered back in 2003 in Dubna, Russia, by a group of scientists led by nuclear physicist, Yuri Oganessian. It was later named Moscovium. I guess they wanted the name associated with the capital, rather than Dubna, a small town which most people outside of Russia would have never heard of."

"I guess Moscovium sounds a little better than Dubnavium," Spire joked.

"That's true!"

"But hang on a minute. Wasn't Lazarus talking about this stuff back in 1989 when he first revealed he'd been reverse engineering flying saucers?" Spire said.

"Exactly! Lazarus claimed that Element 115 was used as some kind of fuel, which had to be cut into slim pyramidal structures, for the anti-gravity propulsion systems the craft used."

Spire was silent for a moment, as he mulled over what Isobel had just told him. "It does tend to lend some credence into what Lazarus was saying back then, if he was talking about a stable Element 115 some 14 years before the existence of Moscovium was announced."

"Exactly," Isobel replied.

"I'll need to do a little more research on all this," Spire conceded.

"Vell, that's what you have me for," Isobel replied.

"Very true. Okay listen, I've a few things to do before bed so I'll say goodnight for now. We can catch up over the next few days. I'll let you have my itinerary as soon as I know it," he said.

"Sounds good, sleep vell Robert," Isobel said, ending the call.

Spire checked the time. It was approaching 9 p.m. and he'd not eaten yet. He wondered into the kitchen and rustled up a simple snack of beans on toast, sprinkled with cheese on top and a good pouring of HP Brown Sauce. He then filled Charlie's bowl full of *Catnips* dried food, looked out into the rear garden again to make sure everything appeared as it should, checked everywhere was secure, and then headed into his bedroom to get ready for bed.

Spire had turned the lights off and was laying in his bed, thinking of Lazarus' seemingly in-depth knowledge of an exotic element called Element 115 back in the 1980's, when it was only officially discovered and added to the periodic table in 2003. It was perplexing to say the least. *Could Lazarus have just foreseen its discovery, or had he really handled the element, allegedly used as alien fuel for a flying saucer whilst working at Area 51?*

Spire must have dozed off for a while, but opened his eyes with an odd feeling of unease. The room was dark, just a narrow shaft of light entering his window through a six-inch gap he'd left between the bottom of the window frame and the blind.

He lay there for a while, wondering why he was feeling concerned, but his thoughts quickly turned to dread as he heard something or someone in his bedroom.

"I didn't expect you to take my advice, Mr Spire when I warned you to back-off investigating this matter, but I must say, I'm impressed with your tenacity," a voice, which sounded oddly familiar, said ominously.

CHAPTER 10

"WHAT THE HELL?" Spire yelled; the sound and tone of his own voice unfamiliar to him, as he tried to leap from the bed, but found he couldn't move. He was paralysed, unable to move any part of his body, apart from his mouth and eyes, slightly. *Am I experiencing some kind of sleep paralysis dream?*

He'd read about the phenomenon, and knew that such dreams caused a temporary inability to move, and occurred right after falling asleep or waking up.

"Don't worry, I am not here to hurt you, and no, you aren't dreaming, but in the morning you'll feel that you had been," the voice said, from somewhere at the end of his bed.

"*Who the hell are you?* How did you get in – Was that you by the shed earlier? My instincts were right, how did I miss you?" Spire said, his heart pumping inside his chest, his limbs feeling like they were made of lead.

"You almost caught me. I was careless, that doesn't usually happen. I have drugged you, but don't worry, you'll not be harmed. It is a paralytic drug based on a botanical pharmaceutical called *Curare*, a plant native to South America.

"What the Fu –?"

"Save your breath. The plant extract was originally used to paralyze animals when being hunted. By the mid-1940s, *Curare* was being used as an adjunct to anaesthesia and in the 1950's researchers began creating synthetic paralytic drugs. Our company however has managed to develop a far more sophisticated and stable version, which renders all muscles in the patient's body useless, whilst having no effect on their diaphragm and ability to breath, or indeed their vocal chords or eyes. This particular drug also contains sodium pentothal, or truth serum, but again, a far more sophisticated version than the drug we've all seen used in Hollywood movies."

"You son-of-a-bitch. What do you want from me?" Spire replied, feeling groggy and helpless in front of his captor.

"No need to be alarmed. I like you Spire, which is why I'm doing this and why you're still alive. I had considered far more, shall we say, archaic methods, to try and get you to talk, but I figured that wouldn't have worked on you anyway," Sentenza said, moving forward into the narrow slither of light, allowing Spire to get a glimpse of him for the first time.

"It's you! From the chapel. You bastard, I should have finished you off when I had the chance," Spire said, feeling himself dribble as he spoke.

Sentenza laughed. "From what I recall it was me who almost finished you off, but I admire your humorous courage."

Spire tried to get up from the bed again, but it was useless, he was frozen to the spot, only able to move his eyes, and breathe.

"Okay, so I need to ask you a few questions. My job is to plug up any leaks, stop the spread of sensitive information. Please tell me what Lazarus told you all before he was killed," Sentenza said.

Spire absorbed the question and felt his mind assimilate the response. Just before he started speaking, he realised he had no real control over what he was saying and he felt Lazarus' final words spill from his lips;

"...I have been searching for the truth all my life, the pursuit of science and continued discovery has been my mantra. I have been lucky enough to be involved in some incredible research, **Project Galileo** being the ultimate research project with which I was involved, with allowed me access to the ultimate truth and technology and, since learning it, I decided to make it my single goal to ensure that at some point, the *world knows about it also, for I feel that it is a continued sin against all of us for the knowledge I am about to share, to be controlled by so few, arguably unworthy people."*

Sentenza's eyes widened as Spire spoke, and he leaned further forward in the chair he was seated on. "Continue," he said softly.

Spire felt his mind whir into action, reciting word for word what Lazarus had said at the presentation.

"...The Industrial Military Complex continues to spend billions of dollars to fund illegal and clandestine military projects, USAP's – Unacknowledged Special Access Projects – the likes of which most people would consider to be pure science fiction if they knew about them. Part of my mission is to bring the age of cover-ups, denial, control and suppression of the masses to an end, and instead, replace it with the age of science, enlightenment, technology and transparency and peace so that humanity can be welcomed into the galactic family of universal consciousness where it truly belongs..."

Spire fought against the fog, trying to prevent the words coming out, but it was no good.

"Film, Roswell film, it looks so real," he heard himself saying.

"Continue," Sentenza ordered.

"...what I can finally prove to you all today, is that we are indeed, not alone, and not only that, but the technology that most of you only thought existed in the realms of science fiction, does indeed exist now, and has done so for decades."

Spire felt his head spinning, before shouting; *"He's gone, the professor has been shot!"*

Sentenza sighed. Lazarus has given away more than he'd thought before his demise. What he'd said hadn't left much to the imagination. "Good, see you can cooperate when asked nicely," he said to Spire, a sly grin forming across his face.

"You know I'm going to kill you when I can finally move," Spire replied.

"Oh, come on Mr Spire, don't be nasty now, I don't like being threatened."

Spire ignored Sentenza's comment.

"So, tell me if you managed to recover Lazarus' smartphone device, has the Russian got it?"

The words flowed from Spire's mouth like water; "Yes we did, and no she hasn't," he said.

"Well that's good for her, and I'm guessing you. At least I no longer need to pay her a visit."

"So, did you manage to gain access to Lazarus' device?"

Spire heard the question and it felt like he was being tickled and had to say *stop*, but instead, had to reply, "Yes."

Spire took in a deep breath, cursing to himself for his inability to control his responses.

"What did you find?" asked Sentenza.

"A...a message," Spire replied.

"Curious, a message for whom?

"For...for me," Spire replied, fighting to try and control his responses.

"Continue, what did the message say?"

Spire thought back to when he was standing in front of the hologram of Lazarus, and then the message came flooding out; *"If you are viewing this image of me, it means my fears have come to pass, and I am no longer around to speak with you myself. I will need to keep this short. Despite the advanced nature of my little cell phone gadget, the holographic recording capability, is of course limited,"*

Spire groaned, trying to fight the words that were forming in his head, but they felt like a recorded message, perfect recall of events he'd witnessed and sounds he'd heard.

"Continue," Sentenza's voice broke through Spire's semi-conscious state.

Spire then heard a more familiar sound in the back of his mind, a faint cry.

But the thoughts and words kept forming. *No!* Spire told himself, but it was no good. *"A project, it's called, The Galileo*

Project. He's talking about Area 51, sometime in the early 1980's. This technology can save us from ourselves and end mankind's reliance on fossil fuels. It would make oil, coal, the fossil fuel economy and the plundering of the Earth's natural resources, a thing of the past. Imagine free, clean, zero point energy from the fabric of space-time for all, and an end to the greatest crisis faced by humanity - global warming." Spire spurted, starting to feel mentally exhausted.

"Interesting, please continue," Sentenza spoke quietly and hypnotically.

"Element...Element 115," Spire muttered.

There it was again. The cry louder and closer this time, and then a loud hiss, followed by a loud meow. It was Charlie!

"Damn cat, get lost," he heard Sentenza growl, through a muffled haze

"Don't you dare...dare, harm him," Spire groaned, his mind suddenly starting to feel a little clearer, his limbs less heavy. Was the drug wearing off?

"Please, answer the question. Continue with describing the message you heard," Sentenza pushed.

Spire's head felt slightly clearer, and he seemed to be able to resist providing an immediate answer to the Asian man's questioning.

"Continue," Sentenza demanded.

"Robert, continue my quest, the truth is out there," was all Spire could think of saying, now able to control his thoughts and conceal the rest of Lazarus' posthumous message.

There was silence in the room for what felt like ages, but in reality it was only seconds. Then Spire heard Charlie cry again from somewhere out in the corridor. As he did, he felt a sudden energy that he'd not felt since he'd heard the voice in the room. Voice? Was there really a voice or had he been dreaming?

Spire sat bolt upright, and with a surge of adrenalin, jumped out of his bed, but, something wasn't quite right. His legs buckled underneath him, and he crumbled to the floor, where he quickly felt a dark cloud envelope him, and then inky blackness.

CHAPTER 11

PARALYTIC DRUGS RELAX the muscles to the point where it's impossible to use most of the muscles of the body, and Spire's largest muscles, his glutinous maximus, leg and calf muscles hadn't yet recovered from the large dose of the truth/paralysis drug that Sentenza had administered, and they'd not been able to support his muscular frame as he'd leapt from the bed.

Spire's sudden surge of energy and movement had proven to be too much and he'd collapsed onto the floor in a heap and, after blacking out, had continued sleeping for another few hours. When he came around, he was disoriented, but a familiar sound quickly brought him to his senses; *meow,* Charlie purred, as he rubbed his head against Spire's cheek.

"Jeez, hello there," he muttered to the cat as he slowly got to his feet. *What an earth had just happened?* was Spire's first thought. He checked the time; his bedside clock was showing, 12.15 a.m.

As Spire headed into the kitchen to get a glass of water, he felt totally confused. He recalled chatting with Isobel on the phone at some point in the evening about Element 115, then shortly after that going to bed, but was that yesterday or earlier? *Had I only been asleep for two to three hours?* Nothing made sense.

Spire ran the tap, filled a glass with cold water and gulped it down in one. *How much brandy had I drunk?* He felt like he had a hangover from hell coming. He poured a second glass and sat down at the kitchen table, trying to gather his thoughts. *"Spoke with Isobel, heard a noise, checked outside...went to bed,"* he muttered to himself. Very slowly he started recalling a very strange dream he'd had, about the shooting, about Professor Lazarus. As he sat there, a feeling of dread slowly enveloped him. The noise he'd heard. Someone *had* been outside after all. Then the penny dropped. *Someone had broken in. Someone had drugged him.*

Spire jumped up and grabbed a kitchen knife from the wooden block on the counter before heading along the corridor and checking the front door. It was secure and locked. He checked the windows in the lounge, all closed and locked. He headed back into the kitchen to try the back door, a slight shiver racing up his spine as he reached for the handle. The kitchen door clicked open, *it was unlocked.* "*Shit,*" Spire whispered, as he realised someone had been in. He never left the rear door unlocked and he recalled locking it after checking outside. Spire grabbed a torch, pulled on a pair of slippers and headed out, checking the garden carefully as he proceeded along the side. The plant pot was upright, where he'd left it. Spire pulled himself up on the fence and he stood on the low wall, and turned to look at the shed, shining the torch on the roof. Then he saw it, the moss that covered the roof showed evidence of being disturbed. The assailant had no doubt been lying; flat down on the angled roof. Spire cursed himself for missing it the first time he'd come out.

He dropped back off the wall and tested the rear garden door, still locked. Anyone with an ounce of strength could get over the wall though.

Spire headed back inside, shivering as he closed and locked the kitchen door. He needed to report the matter to GLENCOM. He guessed he'd been given some kind of truth drug to get him to speak, *but by who and what had he said?*

Spire gave Charlie some water, then grabbed his laptop, poured himself a small Cognac – he'd need it to get back to sleep that was for sure – and powered up his computer, entering the secure area to update Oliver on the night's events. As he did so, he mulled over whether to call Travis to discuss travel arrangements and also alert him as to what had just happened. The only saving grace was that neither he nor Charlie seemed to have been harmed.

The hired white Ford came into view, which Sentenza had parked well over a half a mile from Spire's cottage, nicely hidden near the entrance to a farmer's field. As he jogged back along the quiet country road, his warm breath condensing into streams of white mist in the cold air, he glanced up at the millions of visible stars in the black sky, relatively unaffected by light pollution. *A magnificent sight*, he mused, as he reached the entrance to the farmer's field, and his parked hire car. He pressed the key fob and jumped in, and inserted the key into the ignition.

He'd managed to question Spire for as long as possible. Normally the drug he'd given him would have kept most men talking all night, but Spire had started coming around way earlier than he expected, even factoring in his obvious fitness. He hadn't managed to extract much from him. The main area of interest being the possibility that Lazarus did indeed manage to smuggle some Element 115 out of Groom Lake, *but how?* He knew the CIA had suspected he had some of the elusive element and had been trying to get their hands on it for some time, even raided Lazarus' home.

Sentenza pulled onto the main road. There wasn't much more he could do down here. Neither Spire nor his female friend had Lazarus' device it seemed. He'd inserted a tracker into Spire's smart phone so at least he could keep tabs on him. Spire was certainly an interesting adversary and he had to admire his courage in getting involved in what was the U.S.A. and U.K. Governments' ultimate secret.

Sentenza accelerated along the deserted country road, towards the M4. He'd head back to London, and sleep all morning. He drove off into the night, realising this assignment was proving a lot more interesting than even he imagined.

CHAPTER 12

Las Vegas, Nevada

DEXTER HEADED DOWN to the Flamingo's parking lot situated next to the hotel, exited the elevator and walked the short distance to his black, Ford Mustang. He reached for his keys and depressed the key fob, unlocking the door and also activating the convertible hood, which swiftly retracted, until clunking into placed in its rear compartment. He jumped in the car and turning on the ignition, the powerful V8 erupting to life.

It had only been 24 hours since he'd heard from his friend, Spire, and since then he'd checked out of the Sahara and checked into the Flamingo. He figured he'd get a round of golf in before things started getting busy, which they usually did as soon as Spire was on the scene.

Dexter pulled out of the parking lot onto Linq Lane and entered Flamingo Road. He reached for his sunglasses to shield his eyes from the bright morning sun and filled his lungs with fresh air, well non-artificially conditioned air at least. He pulled onto Nellis Boulevard, and crossed over East Vegas Valley drive. After a short while he spotted a sign for the *Treetops Golf and Country Club* and pulled off the highway. Not long after was driving up a tree-lined road, following signs for *Treetops*. A large, weather-beaten, oak sign pointed the way to the golf club's car park. Dexter slowed down and turned off the road and drove slowly along the well-kept avenue, nicely named *Tee Street*, slowing down to allow a white Porsche Carrera that was coming towards him to pass.

He pulled into the gravel parking area; the vehicle's wide tyre's crunching satisfyingly over the chippings, and pulled into an empty space, next to a black Range Rover and in the shade of a palm tree, and killed the engine. Apart from a few other vehicles, the parking area was empty. *Covid was still keeping the older members away,* he figured.

Dexter removed his sunglasses and got out of the Mustang, sucking in a deep breath of genuine fresh air, before fetching his golf clubs from the trunk.

Dexter headed over to the clubhouse, the large date palms flanking the entrance rustling in the late morning breeze. He didn't usually play golf alone, but today he fancied playing nine holes in solitude; it gave him plenty of thinking and planning time. He'd always been a bit of a drifter, with no real fixed abode. He spent at least four to six months of the year here in Vegas, managing to get great deals on long stays at a number of the resort's hotels. Dexter hated paying utility bills, and by staying at his favourite hotels he made sure he didn't get any. A loss at the tables, whilst not enjoyable, he could take, paying utility bills, he hated more.

Dexter headed into the changing room, found a locker and put on a pair of spiked golfing shoes and headed out a side door, grabbed a golf trolley and headed down a short gravel path to the first Tee.

Since leaving the Marines and retiring, he'd been undertaking 'private' security work, which he found perfectly suited his lifestyle. It enabled him to utilise the skills he'd acquired in the Marines when fighting for his country in Afghanistan and Gulf Wars One and Two. He was fiercely patriotic, but not when it came to ignorant politicians making the wrong decisions and then expecting the armed forces to clean up the mess they'd created.

As he pulled out a driving wedge from his golf bag he wondered what the next four years would bring under a new Presidency. The last four had been a little too crazy, even for him.

Yep, he was more than happy with his lot, being able provided security and 'assistance' for anyone who was prepared to pay for it. Whilst he occasionally broke the law, he wasn't prepared to allow his own moral code to be broken. If anyone had done something bad to someone else or to his country, the perpetrator had it coming to them as far as he was concerned. If someone wanted to pay him to take care of those types of people and problems, then he was available for hire.

Dexter bent down and placed the *Slazenger* ball on the tee and positioned himself for the 450 yard par 4 drive towards the green. He took a practise swing to warm up, stepped forward, looked down at the ball, and then towards the green in the distance, and swung the club. The driver connected squarely and made a satisfying *thwack*, sending the golf ball through the air in a decent arc towards its target.

Dexter placed the club back into his golf bag and headed off along the fairway to find his ball. As he took in the view and relished the peace and tranquillity of the course, he wondered what Spire's next little escapade would bring. UFO's weren't something he'd thought much about, despite hearing some stories / incidents from his days in the military, but he was certainly intrigued by the subject. The research he'd done on the phenomenon had piqued his interest, especially if his government, or rogue elements within it, were covering up such significant truths. He suspected the majority of sightings, if not all, were military in nature. Clandestine projects and advanced technology that was decades ahead of anything in the civilian realm.

Dexter found his ball, pulled a five iron from his bag, lined up the shot and hit the ball. It was another nice shot, which propelled the ball to within sight of the green. As he walked after it, a noise in the trees over to his right caught his attention. He looked over and saw two grey squirrels playing amongst the Date Palms that lined the fairway.

Dexter arrived at his golf ball, pulled out a nine iron and gently hit the ball, lofting it high into an arc, the ball landing on the green fifty feet away with a satisfying *thud*.

He replaced his club, pulled out a putter and walked onto the green. He lined the shot up and took the ten-foot putt. *Perfect*, he thought, as the ball dropped into the hole, moments later.

Dexter collected his *Slazenger* and headed off the green for the path, and towards the second tee, this one 520 yard par 5. As he headed towards the tee, he pondered the evening ahead. A drink in the clubhouse here, followed by a few more back at the hotel casino bar, dinner, and then a few hours of Blackjack sounded ideal.

Dexter took the drive, this time the club face connecting with the ball more to its side, causing an abnormal spin and slicing the ball over to the right of the fairway.

Goddamn, he muttered, as he collected his tee, replaced the club, and headed off once again along the fairway.

Two hours later, Dexter finally reached the ninth tee and performed his final putt of the afternoon, thankful he wasn't continuing on for the remaining nine holes. The round had been enjoyable and the solitude energising. He'd hardly seen a soul on the course, which was a little unusual. Dexter walked the short distance back to the club house, nodded at an elderly couple who were on their way to the first tee and headed into the club house and into the changing rooms where he took a long hot shower.

The time was approaching 4.45 pm when he took a seat at the bar and ordered a Sierra beer.

"Good round sir?" the barman asked.

"Not a bad half round," Dexter replied, gulping down a half bottle of the cold beer.

"Thirsty work all the same," the barman said, as he collected some glasses at the far end of the bar.

"Always good to get into the bar," Dexter said, as he slowly finished the rest of the beer.

"Okay, that's me done," Dexter smiled, as he pulled out a ten dollar note and left it on the bar, telling the barman he could keep the four dollar change.

"Have a good day, sir," the barman said, beaming.

Dexter headed out through the main exit into the late afternoon sun, feeling relaxed and refreshed after the afternoon's exercise. As he emerged into the car park, he noted that the Range Rover had gone and an old, blue Mercedes had parked in its place.

Dexter then saw two, thick-set Mexican-looking men, sitting on the bonnet of the Merc, one with a cigarette smouldering in the corner of his mouth, the other was chewing gum. There was a third man leaning against the passenger door of his car, arms stretched out across the convertible hood. The three of them were laughing, but stopped and stared at him as he headed over.

Here we go, Dexter thought. *Why is it when I have a perfect day, it always gets ruined.*

"This your Mustang my friend?" one of the men, sitting on the Merc, with closely cropped dark hair and long side burns asked, as he tossed his cigarette to the ground.

"Yep, sure is," Dexter replied, as he walked to within fifteen feet of the men and his car.

The man grinned at his friend who was sitting on the Mercedes alongside him, and then spat on the ground. "Very pretty car," he said, in a gruff Mexican accent, as he slid off the hood of the Mercedes.

"I take it you're not here to tend to the greens?" Dexter asked, setting his gold bag down on the ground.

"You guessed right gringo," the man with the sideburns said, smirking.

"My car really doesn't like you leaning on it like that," Dexter said, discreetly checking his immediate surroundings. He didn't really want an altercation right outside the golf club, but he'd probably have little choice. Dexter didn't think it would be a good idea to pull out his *Desert Eagle* from his golf bag and shoot them all, yet. That would bring unwanted attention, and he'd probably end up a Nevada prison for a while until he could get his lawyer sorted out and bail – not a good option.

He hoped that the men didn't have any guns on them, but they'd surely be carrying knives. He felt confident he could take them all on, provided they weren't carrying firearms.

The man who'd slid off the bonnet moved closer to him. "You know why we're here?" he said.

"Hmm, well if it's not to tend to the greens, maybe you've come to check on the drains?"

The other man, still on the bonnet of the Merc, arms folded spat out his chewing gum. "This gringo is a cheeky fuck," he said, as he proceeded to click the knuckles on his right hand.

"No hard feelings gringo, but our boss wants his money back. Money you stole off him in a poker game."

Dexter felt a little confused, but then recalled a private poker game he'd had at one of the casinos a few months back. There had been a slim, Mexican with a nasty scar on his nose in the last round; Dexter had cleaned him out of a good two hundred thousand dollars. He suspected he may have been a gang leader of some kind, drug dealer certainly. "Ah, come to think of it, I vaguely recall," Dexter said, slowly nodding his head.

"Like I said, our boss wants his money back. We will take a hundred in cash, and you can give us the keys to the Mustang now as a down payment," the Mexican, standing six feet in front of him, with the sideburns said.

"It is a *very* pretty car," the Mexican leaning against his car, repeated.

"That's all very interesting. Your boss shouldn't be playing poker if he's such a sore loser, and I did tell you, my pretty car doesn't appreciate Mexicans it doesn't know very well, rubbing their dirty hands all over its nice clean black cloth hood."

The Mexican in front of him pulled out a six-inch blade, which glinted in the sun, and suddenly lunged at him.

Dexter dropped his golf clubs to the ground, gripping the tungsten head of his driver as he did, pulling it clear of the bag. In one fluid motion, he grabbed the shaft of the club and swung the driver around, which connected cleanly with the Mexican's jaw, sending him staggering and spinning six feet to the left and down to the ground. He landed just short of the bonnet of Dexter's Mustang, groaning in a pool of blood.

"Oh dear, I was slicing the ball earlier, but now I'm hooking it," Dexter said, shaking his head.

The other two Mexicans came at him, the guy who'd spat the gum out, lunged at him with a right-handed sweeping punch, which would have knocked most men clean out, had it connected. But Dexter saw it coming a mile off and managed to block the punch with his left forearm, before quickly jabbing the Mexican in the throat with his right fist, crushing his windpipe. The man fell to the ground, clutching his throat in agony.

The third Mexican then came at him, drawing out a long jagged knife from a hidden sheath as he ran. The man's eyes were jet-black, wild looking, as pissed off as anyone could be. Gripping the knife in his right hand, the man frantically swiped it back and forth in front of Dexter's face and torso.

Dexter jumped back, the knife slicing through his shirt on the return swipe. The Mexican thug was fast, but Dexter waited for the right moment to grab his attacker's knife-holding hand.

Dexter's military training gave him the edge in most combat situations, and seeing the moment, he quickly grabbed the man's right wrist, forcing it down and sideways. The move gave him a split second to punch his attacker full on in the nose, twice, which he followed up with a roundhouse kick to the man's left knee cap, breaking it instantly.

The Mexican landed on the ground next to his friend, wailing in agony.

"How much did you say I owed your boss?" Dexter asked, picking up his clubs and composing himself, directing his question at the Mexican who'd demanded the money.

The Mexican spat out blood. "Two hundred thousand dollars, he'll send more of us until you pay."

Dexter placed his boot on the man's thigh and pressed down. "How much do I owe him?"

"Two...two."

"How much?" Dexter shouted, stamping hard on his thigh.

"Argh; stop, stop – nothing, you owe nothing." he finally whimpered.

"Do you two boys agree?"

The men grunted.

"Pardon?"

"Yes...yes, amigo," The Mexican he'd jabbed in the throat, said.

"At last, some common sense," Dexter said, stepping over the man on the floor. "You'd better roll out the way unless you want me to reverse over you," he added, as he placed his clubs back into the trunk.

The men on the floor groaned and started shuffling out of the way, as Dexter got into his car, revved the throaty engine, and slowly reversed. As he did, he made a call to the clubhouse.

The secretary answered after a few rings. "Afternoon, it's Travis Dexter here. I'm just driving out of the club, having played nine holes, but wanted to let you know I was just assaulted by three Mexican thugs in the parking lot."

"Oh, my, I'm...I'm terribly sorry Mr Dexter. Are you okay, can I call an ambulance?" he said, sounding very concerned.

"That might be a good idea, I think two of the Mexicans may need some medical help," Dexter said, as he accelerated down the club's long tree-lined driveway.

"Oh, I see. Got you Mr Dexter, I'll see to that," the club secretary replied, sounding slightly confused.

"Thanks. Have a good day," Dexter said, ending the call, as he turned onto the main road and headed back into town.

CHAPTER 13

Oakdale, West Wales

SPIRE REACHED FOR the phone, still feeling groggy and unable to get back to sleep, anxiety and adrenalin preventing him from doing so. It was now 01.15 and he figured Travis would be free for a quick chat – it being only 5.15 p.m. over there – so he called his number.

After six rings, he heard Dexter's familiar deep voice. "Robert, what the hell, good to hear from you pal. You turned into an insomniac or something?" he asked.

"Spire felt rough, but Travis' familiar voice made him feel a little more secure again. "Hey Travis, good to hear your voice. Yep, you might well ask. I've had a few issues over here, so wanted to call."

"No problem Rob, what's up? I've had a bit of an afternoon of it too. I'll tell you after," Dexter said, the rumble of an engine drowning out the end of his sentence.

"What you doing, cutting the grass?" Spire asked.

"Ha-ha no sorry, I've just pulled into the Flamingo's parking lot. I've got the roof off. Give me a me a few seconds."

Spire waited, a strong gust of wind buffeting the fence in the garden and kitchen window momentarily.

"That's better. Parked up and all yours Robert. So what's up?"

"Where do I start," Spire replied, as he proceeded to tell Dexter the events of the evening, starting off with his call to Isobel earlier on, to waking up on his bedroom floor a short while ago. Spire left no detail out, ensuring Dexter got the full picture.

"Wow, Jesus Robert, this UFO thing is getting pretty serious, very quickly it seems. Sounds like you've been followed since day one of this thing. Whoever broke in managed to slip you some sodium pentothal, get you to reveal what you know. We had a few variants of SP tested on us in the Marines, nasty stuff. Almost impossible to resist letting go of what you know, only the hardiest and well-trained of us managed to overcome the powerful desire to talk during training."

"Well that doesn't fill me with confidence," Spire responded.

"Well, truth be known, the fact you're still alive either suggests your captor liked you or that you didn't reveal too much," Dexter said.

"Gee thanks, I feel better now," Spire replied, taking another gulp of water.

"How'd the stuff get in your system? Did you have a drink before bedtime?"

Spire thought back. "Well, only a Cognac. The usual," Spire said.

"It was probably slipped in there, powder form. It wouldn't take much."

Spire sighed. "Anyway, what happened to you?"

"I ran into a spot of bother at the golf course."

"What happened, a snake find its way onto the green?" Spire joked.

"Yeah how'd you guess, three Mexican snakes actually," Dexter laughed, as he told Spire what had happened.

"Jeez, remind me never to play poker with a Mexican drug baron," Spire said. "There's never a dull moment with you, sounds like you had a worse day than me!"

"You could say that, but hopefully they won't be bothering me again. Listen, I'm about to get into the elevator, what's the plan?" Dexter added.

"Okay, so things are starting to move at a pace here clearly. I think I'm going to head down to *Rendlesham* in a couple of days, take a look at those twin airbases where the purported UFO activity took place back in 1980. I just want to try and speak to a few locals, get a feel for the place, try and find out what actually might have happened. Then, I'll plan the trip over there for next week, and we can hit the ground running in Nevada, perhaps visit the Roswell crash scene and then try and solve the cryptic message Lazarus left for me," he said, suddenly feeling more energised.

"Sounds like a plan. Take it easy though Rob. Are you sure you don't want me to come over there, visit Rendlesham with you?"

Spire thought about it for a moment. "Be good to have you with me, but there's no need, not if we both really need to be out there. Thanks for the offer though, but I'll be fine."

"Yeah, well, keep your wits about you pal. Touch base soon," Dexter said, before ending the call.

CHAPTER 14

Rendlesham Forest, Suffolk, England

RENDLESHAM FOREST IS owned by the U.K's Forestry Commission and consists of around 5.8 square miles of coniferous forest canopy, interspersed with broadleaved belts, heathland and wetland areas. It is located in the county of Suffolk, which is about 8 miles east of the town of Ipswich, on the east coast of the U.K., and around 100 miles or so from the centre of London.

Spire accelerated along the A12, skirting around the town of Ipswich, his Range Rover effortlessly eating up the miles, and the fuel. He had fully recovered from the visit by the mysterious intruder to his cottage in the middle of the night, two nights earlier, and appeared to be suffering no ill effects, apart from a bruised ego.

"I do appreciate you coming with me," Spire said, glancing at Isobel, who was looking elegant but appropriately dressed for a hike in the woods, in her denim jeans, grey Nike trainers and white woollen jumper.

"No problem, I'm beginning to think you might need a bodyguard with you. I can help with zat," she said, shrugging her shoulders.

"Ha-ha, well you might be right there. I seem to be losing my touch a bit," Spire replied, seriously thinking he was starting to get a little old to deal with all the somewhat hazardous tasks GLENCOM sent him on. Assignments that always seemed innocent enough, until reality unfolded and events turned literally globally significant.

"So, vot is the plan when we get to the forest?"

"I'm not entirely sure! But, I want to go and see the location where the UFO supposedly landed, which shouldn't be hard as apparently there's a trail that now leads there, and believe it or not, the location is actually marked on *Google Maps*."

"No vay?!"

"We've also got a meeting with an old chap, used to be a logger in the forest. GLENCOM tracked him down and he's happy to talk to us. Then, hopefully we can have a snoop around the old airbase."

"Oh, exciting, but is that legal? You're kidding about the UFO landing site being marked on the map, right?"

"Well, walking around in the forest is still legal the last time I checked," Spire smiled, as he pulled out to overtake a slow-moving truck.

Pulling back over, he noticed a sign for the *Bentwaters Cold War Museum*, 5 miles distant, a reminder that things must have looked a hell of a lot different back in 1980 when both the Bentwaters and Woodbridge air bases were occupied by U.S. forces as part of the West's cold war deterrent against the Soviet Union.

As they drove along the edge of the forest, he could see the area must have changed massively. Bentwaters had now been turned into a retail park, with a museum instead of fighter-jet filled runways, and the quiet village of Woodbridge, which nestled alongside the forest, had the usual quaint pubs, pizza parlours and takeaways that lined the streets of almost every village, town and city in the U.K.

"I was amazed myself, but here, take a look," Spire said, switching his Sat-Nav screen to *Google* Satellite Maps and zooming in on their current location and the forest. He had some difficulty finding it, but then found the annotation.

"No vay, that's funny of *Google* to mark the landing spot."

"It made me smile," Spire said, as they headed past the football club and onto Woodbridge Road. Pine forest stretched out as far as they could see on their right, and rolling fields with more forested area on their left.

"Where's the air base then?" asked Isobel.

"Woodbridge is just over to our right I think. We should be able to see the end of the runway shortly. We need to take right turn somewhere along here," he said, slowing down.

Spire found the narrow road that intersected the forest and made a right turn. Half a mile later and the far end of the air base's disused runway came into view, cutting a swathe of asphalt through the middle of the forest. "There's the runway," Spire said, nodding to his right side.

"It all looks very desolate out there now. So where are ve meeting this contact?" Isobel asked.

"Not far from here, there's a small café," Spire replied, continuing past the airfield and onto another periphery road. They reached the junction. The alleged UFO landing spot was in the forest somewhere off to the right, the café where they were meeting the contact, a few miles further on, towards Butley Priory. He turned right and continued along the narrow road, forest stretched out on their right side and open farm land to the left. About a mile past the priory Spire saw a sign for a toilet stop area and a small café, called the *Wandering Lamb Café*.

"Here we are," Spire said, pulling into the parking area. He suddenly noticed another SUV, a black Bronco, with blacked-out windows, which had appeared on the main road from nowhere turned in after him, pulling into a space a short distance away.

Spire killed the engine. "Vot's this guy look like, any idea?" Isobel asked, as she dropped the vanity mirror down and checked on how she looked.

"Well he was around twenty-five at the time of the incident so he's going to be sixty-five odd now."

They both got out the car, as they did; an open back red pick-up pulled into the car park and pulled up. A guy with a cap, wearing a green jumper and armless grey jacket jumped out. He looked fit, but had a lined face, perhaps from years of being out in the sun. "I think that might be our guy," Spire said.

Sure enough the old chap headed towards them and said, in a hoarse voice, "Robert Spire, by any chance?"

"Hey, that's me. William Trent I assume?" Spire said, extending his hand and shaking the guy's hand. "Crikey, you've not lost your woodcutter grip," Spire joked.

"Aye, that's true," he said.

"This is my colleague, Isobel; she's an astrophysicist, and part of the team."

Trent smiled and shook her hand too. "Shall we go in for a drink? Don't want to hang around here too long," Trent said, suddenly appearing a little edgy.

"Sure, come on. Let's go inside," Spire said, gesturing for Trent to lead the way into the café.

The three of them headed in and waited to get shown a seat. A sign on the door confirmed that no masks were needed. Some normality had finally returned to rural U.K. following the vaccine roll-out and significant reduction in transmission of the COVID-19 virus that followed.

A waitress showed them to a table near the rear of the basic, but clean, café and Spire ordered some drinks, sparkling water for Isobel and coffees for himself and Trent.

"So, I just want to thank you for agreeing to talk to us today. I assume GLENCOM obviously filled you in on why we are here?"

Spire knew that Oliver had used the recent assassination of Professor Lazarus as an excuse to track down, and speak with the woodcutter, on the basis he remain anonymous, and in order to shine new light on the *Rendlesham* story, from a witness who'd so far remained silent about the events.

"No problem. I'm doing it as long as my name isn't given out. I heard about the assassination of the physicist in London, and felt pretty disgusted by it all. If I can help shed light on things, then I'll feel a little happier I've done my bit," Trent said, speaking in hushed tones.

"That's very good of you," Spire said, glancing at Isobel, and then back to the woodcutter. "So, ready when you are. Provided you're happy, tell us what you know."

"Do you mind?" Isobel said, placing her smartphone down on the table and setting it to *record* mode.

"No that's fine, like I said, as long as I can't be identified," Trent said, his lined face wizened and tired-looking, but his blue eyes still bright and full of life. "So, back in 1980 I was working as a forester in Rendlesham here, started in 1977 and continued in that job until 1988 I believe. Many people confuse the role of a forester with that of the logger, but my job not only concerned the harvest of sustainable timber, but also with the ecological management of Rendlesham Forest and surrounding area. My work took in very close proximity to the U.S. base, and over time I got to know a couple of the boys from the army, mainly the young guards who would patrol the East Gate of the base," Trent paused and seemed to go off in daze for a few seconds.

"Aye, I recall the *F-4 Phantoms* and *A10 Thunderbolts* they kept here, tank busters the yanks called them. An enemy could shoot the hell out of those things and the pilot would still be able fly back to base and land them safely," Trent said, taking a gulp of coffee.

"Fantastic planes," Isobel agreed.

"Must have been pretty noisy at times I guess," Spire said.

"Oh yes, you'd know when the planes were being scrambled. Anyway, I digress," Trent said, putting his coffee cup back down. "So, I knew some of the lads who were on guard duty on the East-Gate, it was right at the end of the runway, and backed onto the forest, which we all now know was where the first sightings of the strange lights in the forest were seen," he said, nervously looking around the café, before his eyes settled back onto Spire and Isobel.

Isobel checked that her phone was still recording, as Trent continued talking.

"One of the guys, I'll not reveal his name, but it's pretty much common knowledge now, was on duty late that night on 29 December 1980. He recalled the night because it was the last night of his midnight shift before he was due to go on his three-day break. Anyway, he was on duty at the East-Gate and he suddenly saw what he thought might be a fire in the forest. He immediately alerted his acting commander and the Deputy Base Commander, who instructed him to check out the situation. He jumped into one of the Jeeps, picked up one of the sergeants on duty, and they drove into the forest to meet with some other patrols already at the location. As they approached, a group of airmen rushed out of the forest, scared as hell by all accounts, said they'd seen a bright light which was surrounded by a strange yellow mist. The guys were then instructed to round up more personnel and collect some light-alls – powerful army generator-powered lights. As they drove back to Woodbridge, through the country roads, my chap told me he had to warn his sergeant buddy to drive carefully because there was a lot of commotion with the wildlife; deer and rabbits were running all over the place and out of the forest."

Trent leaned in to them both. "That got me wondering. See I've chopped many a tree down with a petrol chainsaw and whilst you might get a good few birds in the immediate vicinity scattering, I'd never see animals in flight as described by the airmen that night."

"Go on," Spire said, finishing his coffee.

"Well seems like all hell was breaking loose from what he told me. There were men everywhere, zero supervision, problems with the light-alls failing and the Jeep's vehicle engines cutting out. The men were arguing as to whether they had fuel in the Jeeps or not.

"Intriguing," Spire commented.

"It was then that the Deputy Base Commander arrived and selected several officers, including my contact, to accompany him on a search for the lights, or object that had been seen. As they moved through the forest, equipped with a Starscope – an image intensifier, and a hand-held tape recorder, they apparently found the alleged landing site of whatever the object was and also detected higher than normal radiation levels there. Not long after, they encountered a red orb moving through the forest and other lights in the sky. The base commander's recording of the event can be found on the internet," Trent added.

Spire nodded. "I have listened to it, fascinating I must say."

Trent looked around the café and hesitated before continuing. He leaned in closer, speaking very quietly. "Well yeah, but here's the thing, what I haven't told anyone is that I was also out in the forest that night, checking on a large owl house I'd put up at the edge of the forest, about half a mile from the East Gate. I know, it sounds kind of cheesy, but my son was doing a school project on owls at the time and I was keen on helping him. Anyway, as I was standing there, looking up at the tree the owl house was attached to, I started to hear some distant shouts and car engines, which seemed odd, and given the time it was. I now know this was the noise from the Jeeps. Then, from the directions of the Atlantic, I watched in amazement as two bright orange /white lights streaked in, hell of a speed, and stopped on a dime. At first I thought it must have been a couple of *Phantom* jets flying back from a training mission, but then I realised there was no sound and obviously no jet can simply stop like that and hover."

"Wow! What happened then?" Spire asked, his eyes darting over to Isobel, who was now staring intently at Trent.

"Well, I ran through the wooded area a little distance to where I knew there was a clearing, which gave me a good line of sight towards RAF Bentwaters and the WSA," Trent continued.

"WSA?" Spire repeated.

"The weapons storage area, for the nukes."

"How do you know it vos the WSA you were looking at?" Isobel asked.

Trent paused and looked worried.

"Are you okay?" Spire asked.

"Yes, sorry, the Russian accent just made me nervous."

"Don't worry, we're not back in the 1980's now and Isobel is working with us on this, she one of the good guys," Spire said, patting Trent on his forearm to reassure him.

"It's okay, what the hell can anyone do to me now anyway?" Trent said, sounding a little more confident.

"I know it was the WSA, because you can still see the row of earth-covered bunkers to this day where the nukes were stored."

"Okay, interesting. We can go and have a look after," Spire said to Isobel.

"So, these two lights, they were hovering over the WSA and then suddenly, a beam of light shot down to the ground from one of the objects and seemed to be scanning the ground around the WSA. As I watched in awe, I got the feeling that the light wasn't just a light, it was a blue / white light, intense and almost, well the overriding feeling I had when looking at it was that it was gathering information. Don't ask me why I thought that, I just did."

Spire looked at Isobel, then back at Trent.

"The light then moved over the forest and as strange as it sounds, I saw what looked like a green molten liquid falling out of the light. This went on for a few minutes. The light then just blinked out and the lights in the sky streaked away from the direction they'd come. It was incredible, that's what I saw," Trent said, looking up at them both, his right fingers nervously crimping and fiddling with his shirt cuff on his left wrist.

The three of them sat there in silence for a few seconds, before Spire spoke. "That's pretty incredible William. What do you think you were witnessing?"

Trent looked up at them both, his face pale, each wrinkle looking as if it carried a hundred worries. "I think that the UFOs were somehow gathering information about the weapons being stored there, and not only that," he said, his voice lowering in tone once again, "Not only that, but I think they somehow deactivated the weapons, stop us from being able to use them. That was the rumour going around amongst the men guarding the East Gate when I spoke with them after."

CHAPTER 15

WILLIAM TRENT SUDDENLY became very nervous and had started to noticeably perspire, despite the cool air inside the café. "Listen, if that's all, I really must get back. If you decide to go near the old base, just be careful," he warned, as he got up and hurried for the exit and walked out of the door.

"Vow, what brought that on?" Isobel asked, as she watched the woodsman through the window hurrying over to his parked pick-up.

"No idea, but he was pretty nervous about something."

"Vot do you think about his story?" she asked.

"Well, if true, incredibly interesting. It's not the first time I've heard about what seems to be obvious connections with UFO sightings and nuclear bases."

"Really? Which others do you know about?" Isobel asked.

"Well, it's widely known that back in 1967, missile maintenance crews camping out at Malmstrom Air Force Base in the USA, where the Air Force kept its cold war contingent of Minuteman ICBM nuclear missiles, saw a red, glowing UFO hovering over one of the missile silos. Shortly after, ten missiles went off alert, meaning they were inoperable. *Captain Robert Salas* is on record confirming the events. And that wasn't an isolated incident," Spire said.

Isobel shook her head. "I am aware of a similar incident happening in the former Soviet Union, now Ukraine in 1982, where a disc-shaped UFO was spotted hovering over the nuclear missile silos located there. Instead of shutting the missiles down however, the opposite happened and the UFO seems to have activated one of the missiles, almost initiating World War Three. After fifteen hair-raising seconds, the missile's launch controls re-set to the normal position."

Spire shook his head. "More than a little worrying. Do you get the feeling that beings of a slightly higher intelligence than us might be telling us, figuratively speaking, not to play with matches?"

Isobel shrugged. "It seems that way, and who would blame them."

The waitress appeared and Spire asked for the bill. She brought it thirty seconds later and he left a ten pound note, which included a small tip for the three drinks. "Come on; let's go take a closer look at the alleged UFO landing spot, and the base shall we?"

"Sure, sounds fun, let's go," Isobel replied, as they both got up and left the café.

Outside, the parking lot was pretty much empty, just a couple of vehicles remained, including the black Bronco which had pulled in straight after them. Spire also noticed the obvious set of tyre marks from Trent's pick-up. He'd not only left the café in hurry, but the parking lot too.

Spire pulled out onto the main road and they headed back towards the forest, following the Sat-Nav directions towards the marked UFO landing site location.

Four miles in the opposite direction, William Trent was almost home and approaching a main T-junction. He needed to make a left turn, and his rural home he shared with his wife – and once his son before he'd moved out fifteen years ago – was a mile or so further along the road. As he approached the junction he began to feel a little less apprehensive about the meeting he'd just had. He was glad to have gotten what he knew about the strange incident all those years ago, off his chest, but nevertheless, he still felt nervous talking about the events he'd witnessed over forty years ago.

He applied the brakes, but the servo-assisted hydraulic brake pedal slammed against the foot-well, completely loose and devoid of any pressure or hydraulics. *"What the hell?"* Trent shouted, as he frantically pumped the brake pedal, which was as floppy as a rag doll. An icy chill raced up his spine as the T-junction approached at fifty miles an hour.

The time it took Trent to travel the distance from the moment he realised he had no brakes, to the T-junction, was three very long seconds. His life flashed by in his mind in slow motion as he raised his arms to his face in terror, as he realised at the very least, he'd plough through the hedge that bordered the main road opposite, and into the adjoining farmer's field. If that had happened he might have had a chance. But it was the slow moving tractor that was approaching from the left that got him. The last thing Trent saw was a green blur as his pick-up collided with the steel lifting forks of the tractor at just under fifty miles an hour. The impact crushed the bonnet and forced the engine into Trent's legs, severing them at the knees, before the sudden collision flipped what was left of his vehicle into the air, over the tractor, and finally into the field, where Trent momentarily realised he'd come to rest...forever.

Five miles away, Spire slowed down and pulled over into a small clearing off the road, alongside Rendlesham Forest. A walk through the pine trees to the alleged UFO landing site would feel a little more atmospheric than pulling up in a public carpark and following signs along a purposely designed footway to the site, he reasoned.

"We're going to walk through the forest?" Isobel queried.

"Yeah, why not? At least we can get a little feel for the forest, like the men from the base had that night."

"Fair enough, except that it's daytime, thankfully," Isobel added, getting out the car.

"Well yes. I must admit, I wouldn't really fancy walking through here in the night," Spire admitted.

"Ditto," Isobel said.

"Come on, let's go. We need to walk due south-east for a mile or so and we should reach the spot," Spire said, locking the car.

The pair of them headed into the pine forest, the daylight quickly dimming the deeper they walked in.

There had been no rain for at least six days and the forest floor was dry. As they walked, the occasional small twig snapped under their feet, the sound resonating through the trees.

"I assume there's no bear or wolf in here," Isobel asked, as they walked towards the landing site.

"Only a few brown bear I believe, released by the National Trust a few years ago. They're thriving apparently," Spire replied.

Isobel stopped. "You're bloody kidding me right?"

Spire didn't reply for a few seconds, before saying; "Calm down, yes, I'm kidding. No bears or wolf in the U.K."

"*Khristos,* you had me worried for a bit. They still have plenty in other parts of Europe," she said.

They continued walking, the forest completely still and tranquil, apart from their own footfall. A large bird, somewhere up in the tree canopy made itself known, and flew off from where it had been perched. Another sound, forty feet away from them caused them both to look. "Just a squirrel I think," Spire said.

"You can understand anyone getting spooked in here, especially if they started seeing odd lights, no matter where the lights originated from," Isobel said.

"You're not buying into the lighthouse theory too are you?"

"You mean the Orford Ness Lighthouse that some sceptics suggest the men saw that night?"

Spire nodded, as he checked the ground in front of him, which had suddenly become a little uneven.

"It's a nice explanation, I mean the voice of the Deputy B.C. on the tape recording does seem to coincide with the revolution of the lighthouse's light, but we all know the beam from the lighthouse is white, not red or orange. I also did some research on this and it seems the original tape recording was about four hours long. The public segment last only 18 minutes, and there is suggestion that this segment was released because the pulsating light being witnessed, does in the small 18 minute segment coincidently match up with the rotating beam of the lighthouse. There is also suggestion that the D.B.C's voice is slightly higher in pitch than in other parts of the tape, meaning the tape could have been speeded up a little to ensure the lights being observed by the men, and the rotating lighthouse beam match up. It doesn't make sense that a number of men charged with guarding a nuclear weapons base could mistake a lighthouse for unusual lights in the forest. Neither does it explain what they say they saw in the sky, or how a lighthouse could be responsible for emitting beams of light down to the ground," Isobel said.

"I'm impressed. I had no idea you were so familiar with the technical aspects of the released tape, but something strange certainly seems to have happened that night," Spire added, as he assisted Isobel down into a steep bowl-like depression in the forest.

Spire checked the compass on his smart phone. The electronic dial was spinning erratically as if it were malfunctioning, before finally settling. "That's odd, it's never done that before," he said, as he focused on the screen and the small red arrow tip, as he turned it towards the south-east.

"I have not seen that either," Isobel confessed, screwing her face up. "Are there any electricity power lines nearby I wonder? Or possibly iron-rich rocks, which can be magnetised," she added.

Spire shrugged. "It's possible, a little odd though. It seems to be working okay now," he said, pointing in the direction they needed to go.

He pocketed his phone and the pair of them continued walking for another ten minutes or so, before the trees started to thin out a little.

Suddenly an odd buzzing sound from above startled them. "Did you hear that?" Spire asked, looking up into the tree canopy.

"I did," Isobel whispered, looking up, but seeing nothing.

The sound faded in an out, like a distant swarm of bees which appeared to be above them somewhere. "Very curious," Spire said, scanning the trees around them. They moved on. Suddenly a thin beam of blue light could be seen on the trunk of a tree ten feet or so from where they were standing. *"Do you see that? What the hell is it?"* Spire said, now feeling somewhat anxious as he looked up to try and see where the light was coming from.

"I don't like this, let's get the hell out of here," Isobel whispered, grabbing Spire's wrist.

"I agree, come on, follow me," Spire said, as they started jogging though the trees towards the lighter, less dense area of forest ahead of them.

CHAPTER 16

THEY'D ONLY BEEN jogging for ten seconds or so before they heard some voices, kids shouting.

"Where is it you *idiot*, I told you it was too close to the tree-tops," a boy's voice shouted.

"It was fine, but then I lost control," another shouted.

From the clearing, two teenage boys came running into the forest, one holding some kind of control unit hanging from a strap around his neck.

"Hey!" Spire shouted, quickly realising what he and Isobel had just seen, and what the kids were searching for. "You guys looking for your drone?"

"Yeah, we were flying it just above the forest a minute ago and lost control."

"Has it got some kind of laser lights fitted to it?" Spire asked, breathing heavily.

"Yeah, it's a UFO drone, cool eh?" The kid with the control unit around his neck said, with a cheeky grin.

Isobel looked at Spire and then back at the kids. "You guys need to be a bit more damn careful with that thing."

"Sorry," the kid said, before the pair of them ran deeper into the woods in search of their toy.

"Jeez, this whole thing is giving me the jitters," Spire said, as he watched the boys vanish into the trees. "Come on, the *real* UFO landing spot must be just over there," he said, pointing to a dark object just visible through the trees, resting in a small clearing, which some hikers were standing around and appeared to be studying.

Spire and Isobel walked into the clearing and the location of supposed December 1980 landing site of the UFO. It was a replica of the object which was allegedly seen by some members of the USAF, which had landed at this very spot.

Spire nodded and said hello to the three hikers who were also studying the black, triangular-shaped replica craft, resting on the forest floor.

"One of the men that night supposedly touched it, ran his hand along the object which he described as like smooth, black glass. As he did so, he has now revealed that he experienced some kind of binary telepathic download, or zeros and ones."

"I think I recall reading that somewhere too. It always struck me a little odd that it took so long for the airman to reveal that vital part of the encounter." Isobel said, looking at him in slight disbelief.

"Seems very farfetched I know, but this entire thing does, so I'm not ruling anything out at this point."

"I still find it fascinating that the forestry, or whoever it is, has gone to the trouble to place a model of the object that supposedly landed here."

"Anything to get the tourists here, eh?" Spire said.

Isobel smiled.

The pair of them studied the craft for a while, before Spire noticed a small group of people heading along the path towards them. "Come on, I've seen enough, let's get back to the car and explore the base."

CHAPTER 17

RAF Woodbridge
Suffolk, England

SPIRE AND ISOBEL made their way back through the forest without incident and jumped back into the Range Rover.

"Well, that was fun. I could have killed those kids," Isobel said, as she clipped her seat belt in.

Spire shook his head and smiled. "Just shows, it's easy to get spooked when you've got things on your mind, especially in an unfamiliar setting."

"Come on, let's go check the base over and get back to civilization," Isobel added.

Spire tapped the ignition button, and the Range Rover's engine roared into life, and he pulled off from the verge and headed towards the disused airbase. Spire turned into the road they'd driven along before, this time, the end of Woodbridge Base, and the disused runway was on their left.

"How are we actually going to get in?" Isobel asked.

"I'm not quite sure yet, but I'm sure we'll find a way," Spire replied, as he found an overgrown lane which led off the main road and up towards the old base. Poking out above the trees and through the overgrown foliage, some of the old grey decaying buildings could just about be seen. He drove up the overgrown lane as far as he could, and parked under some low hanging trees, his vehicle pretty much concealed from the road. "Looks like this is about as far as we can go," he said.

Ahead of them was a chain-link fence, some twelve feet high, with rolls of barbed wire running along the top of it.

The fence was secured by thick concrete posts set into the ground at ten-foot or so intervals.

"Come on, let's go take a look," Spire said, grabbing a flashlight from the glove compartment.

Isobel gave him an apprehensive look, before getting out the car.

They both proceeded on foot, through the overgrown boundary area, where nettles and weeds had grown out of control, and up to the edge of fence. From where they were standing they had a clear view of the cracked runway and what must be the old bunkers and hangers.

"Well, not exactly the Savoy now is it?" Isobel said, staring at the huge, derelict site.

"Don't worry, I don't plan on booking us in," Spire replied, heading left along the fence, looking for any way to get inside.

After ten minutes of walking through the bushes and nettles that lined the rough ground, Spire spotted something. "There," he said, pointing to an area of fencing close to the next concrete pillar. He went over to inspect it. The concrete had badly corroded and the fence had become detached from the pillar. Spire grabbed the fence and yanked it back. The fence gave way and more of it ripped away from the concrete it had been set into. He continued pulling at it until he'd created a large enough hole for them both to crawl through.

They carefully crawled through the damaged section of fence and into the base.

A little distance away, a black Bronco pulled off the road and stopped. The same black Bronco that had been at the *Wandering Lamb Café* earlier. Two men jumped out wearing dark clothing and black padded jackets. Both were wearing ear pieces and looked like they were from the military. The man on the left, with dark hair, whose name was Briggs, but went by the codename of Hawk, had an army-style 'buzz-cut' and was speaking quietly into the mic on his collar. "Apollo team to Control, we are following the targets into Woodbridge. Yes, it's the same couple from the chapel in Greenwich. He's with the Russian. Affirmative, they won't be leaving the base, you can be sure of that." Briggs said, as he nodded to his colleague.

His colleague, a fair-haired, tough-looking, square-jawed ex-military type, with cold, steely blue eyes, codename Condor, nodded back. They moved slowly up to Spire's Range Rover, using it for cover, before tracing the route Spire and Isobel had taken a short while earlier.

CHAPTER 18

THE WOODBRIDGE RAF base, had until 1993 been leased to the United States Air Force, and since 2006 has been split up into two parts, Woodfield Airfield and the Rock Barracks. The old base was still used as training for the Army Air Corps and Spire guessed they'd breached the fence into the airfield section. Spire had read that the MOD had announced the base would close fully in 2027, where the land would no doubt be used to build new residential housing, or another retail park. There would be little evidence left of the twin, cold war air bases, and certainly no trace of the atmosphere that would have existed during the height of the cold war, and the night of December 29th 1980.

Spire and Isobel hugged the fence line as they proceeded deeper into the base and on towards what looked like some kind of guard post, the concrete grey structure visibly deteriorating and crumbling, steel rebar exposed in a number of places. Painted on the side of the building was a large, faded mural for which the Americans are famous. The artwork usually varied between simple, rough graffiti to full-blown works of art, usually connected with the USAF. This one was of a faded, Fairchild Republic, A-10 *Tank-buster* aircraft.

"Nice artwork," Spire said, pointing out the mural. "A-10 *Tank-busters* or *Warthogs* as they were known. It was one of the most formidable aircraft in the USAF arsenal at the time. Had your countrymen decided to invade Europe, they'd have faced the full wrath of these things," Spire said, as he admired the mural. "They were equipped with one of the most powerful cannons ever flown at the time; could rip a tank to shreds with their depleted armour-piercing uranium shells. I think the gun could fire at an astonishing rate of 3000 rounds a minute," Spire added, recalling his interest in war planes from when he was younger.

Isobel smiled. "The plane was actually designed to fit around the powerful *Avenger* rotary cannon, which could actually fire at 3,600 rounds a minute," Isobel corrected.

Spire was a little taken aback. "And how would you know that?"

"I'm a scientist don't forget, and Russian. Part of my training was to learn about American war technology from the 1960's to the present day."

Spire raised his eyebrows. "I'm impressed," he said, as they walked around the back of the building, finding the entrance. He looked into the gloomy space, just a square building with two small windows covered with rusting iron bars and inside, crumbling plaster painted a faded yellow. There were a few old, empty crates stacked in one corner, and another mural, this time of the silhouette of a black tank with a red target painted over it, the words *Tank-buster* written underneath.

"Looks like an old ammunition or storage building," Spire said.

Isobel peered in.

"Come on, let's move on," Spire suggested.

They both continued further into the base, sticking pretty much to the fence line. About one hundred feet away was a large rectangular building, sunk partially into the ground and with sloping grass-covered sides which rose to the flat concrete roof. It had to be a bunker or perhaps command post of some kind, Spire assumed. "Over there, come on," he said.

They reached what was either the front, or rear of the building which consisted of a solid wall of concrete. They were standing on a concrete slab, but in the left-hand corner, was a small rectangular opening, with rusty, steel steps leading down to what looked like another platform, strewn with rubbish.

"Yuck," Isobel said, looking down.

"This looks like a possible entrance, come on," Spire said, pulling his flashlight out and shining it down the stairwell.

"Are you serious?" Spire was already halfway down the steps and didn't hear Isobel's protestation. She followed him down.

Three-hundred feet behind, the two men from the Bronco reached the guard building / storage silo, and looked on through compact, high-powered binoculars, as their targets descended out of site.

CHAPTER 19

THE BUILDING APPEARED to be an old command post, or bunker of some kind. At the bottom of the stairwell and beyond the rubbish that had been dumped over the years was a set of steel doors. Spired walked up to it and shone the flashlight. He could see a steel chain and padlock wrapped around the curved door handles. "Damn, looks like it's locked," he said, as he reached out to yank the chain. As he did, he was amazed to find that the padlock, although locked, wasn't actually securing the chain. It had been locked in place, but not locking the chain to the door. The chain unravelled from the door handle and clattered to the ground in a heap. "That's odd, so much for security," Spire said.

"Maybe it was done in a rush and someone made an error," Isobel suggested.

Spire yanked on the door and it slowly creaked open, letting out a pungent, damp, musky odour.

He reached into his pocket and pulled out two Covid-19 hospital face masks and handed one to Isobel. "Here, these things might be handier than I thought. Don't worry, it's a new one," he said.

They both put on the masks which helped block out the unpleasant odour, before heading inside, Isobel making sure the door was wedged open with a broken piece of crate she found on the floor.

Spire shone the torch around. They were at the start of a long, wide corridor. Fixed to the left hand wall was a stainless steel plaque, and stencilled on it in black lettering was written;

67th Aerospace Rescue and Recovery Squadron - ARRS

"ARRS," Spire slowly read out.

"The 67th Air Rescue and Recovery Squadron I think moved here from *Morón Air Base*, in Spain, in 1970. They were assigned an air rescue and special operations mission, and were responsible for locating and recovering, amongst other things, NASA space capsules, should they splash down in the North Atlantic area. It was one hypothesis for what the men saw that night, an accident with an experimental lunar capsule, which fell into the forest and had to be recovered."

Spire looked at Isobel, her attractive features illuminated by his flashlight. "Are you sure you're not a Russian spy?" he half-joked. "Your knowledge on this stuff is never ending."

Isobel smiled. "Like I said, we had to study all these...events," she shrugged.

"Hmm," Spire said, unsure whether to fully believe her. "Come on, let's go further inside."

The cone of light from Spire's torch revealed a maze of vaults and rooms with enormous solid steel doors, many with elaborate combination locks.

"It sure is spooky in here," Isobel whispered.

Even with their masks on, the complex had the nauseating odour of stale air, no doubt due to the building having been sealed for a long period of time.

"We shouldn't wander in too far. If we get locked in or fall and injure ourselves we'll be in trouble," Isobel whispered.

Spire pulled out his smartphone. Isobel was right; they had no phone signal in here. They had no contact with the outside world inside the building, a thought that made Spire nervous.

They continued along the corridor, the sliver of light from the slightly ajar entrance door growing dimmer and dimmer. They came across an open door and Spire shone the torch inside. They were standing at the threshold to a small room which looked like it was some kind of communications room.

One entire wall was fitted out with an old telephone system. "Jeez, that looks ancient," Spire commented.

"The MOD used the oldest system they could get away with; it was more efficient and could not be hacked into," Isobel said.

As they studied it, they heard a *clunk,* resonate along the corridor, the origin of the sound hard to pin point.

"*Christos,* what was that?" Isobel whispered, looking at Spire, her eyes wide with concern.

The pair of them froze for a moment, before heading back out into the corridor to check. The door at the end was still open, a shaft of light spilling into the underground facility.

"Maybe it was an animal or something? God knows there must be so many old pipes or things that can go clank under here," Spire whispered.

"I don't feel comfortable down here," Isobel admitted.

"No, I don't either. Let's just check out the end of the corridor and we can head back out," Spire suggested.

They walked further along the main corridor and reached the end, the narrow sliver of light from the open door now barely visible at the far opposite end. There were two doors and Spire tired the handle of the door on the right. It opened onto another narrow corridor, and a little further down, Spire's flashlight caught a sign on the left side with the words, *DECON 1.* They walked further in, carefully avoiding debris and broken crates on the floor until they reached the room beneath the sign. Spire shone the light inside to reveal a small cubicle with a shower unit. Further along the corridor were three more decontamination units, *DECON 2, 3 and 4.*

"God forbid, in the event of a nuclear attack, personnel would have been required to take an external shower and go through decontamination procedures before they could enter the main complex," Isobel whispered.

Further along the corridor they could see what appeared to be vents. Opposite *DECON 4* was another room, with row upon row of decaying telephone switchboards and equipment.

"I think we've seen enough," Spire said, turning to Isobel. As he did, his foot came into contact with something on the floor, a can of some kind, which he accidentally kicked. The noise echoed along the corridor, causing Isobel to jump and grip him tightly.

"Sorry, that was me," Spire said, shining the flashlight to the ground, which picked up an old can of *Esso* fuel.

"I mean it, let's go," Isobel said, gripping spire's hand tightly.

As Spire led Isobel back along the pitch-black corridor, he thought back to the nuclear attack government information programmes, that he vaguely recalled seeing as a child, which advised citizens on how to protect themselves from such an attack. He recalled advice on removing doors inside the house and hiding under kitchen tables and such like. The suggestions seemed completely preposterous in comparison to the relative protection afforded by concrete and steel bunkers such as this one. The general public, most of humanity would have zero prospects in the event of a nuclear war.

The ever brighter shaft of light from the open door at the end of the long corridor dragged Spire from the sombre thoughts.

As they headed towards the exit, the pair of them both starting walking faster, as if some invisible, involuntary force was pulling them towards the light, and then, as they were about fifteen feet from the door, it slammed closed, with a loud metallic, *thud.*

CHAPTER 20

SPIRE AND ISOBEL panicked, and Spire ran the last ten feet and at the door, slamming into it with his shoulder. The door flung open with little effort and Spire flew out onto the small external platform, falling into the heap of rubbish, the door slamming against the outside wall.

It appeared the wedge had slipped away from underneath the steel door and the door had then been blown closed by the wind. "*Christos!* I nearly had a heart attack," Isobel shouted, helping Spire up from the floor.

"Thanks," he said, brushing himself down. "I did get a little concerned then, I must be honest."

Isobel shook her head. "Come on, let's get out of this base, I've had had enough."

Spire nodded and they both ascended the steel steps back to ground level. "We'll head back via that elevated mound over there," Spire pointed to a cracked asphalt area towards what appeared to be the first of at least twenty raised mounds in the ground. "I think those must be the WSA's," he said.

"The nuke silos?" Isobel queried.

Spire nodded.

"Okay, a quick look, and then we get the hell out, agreed?"

"Agreed," Spire nodded.

They both jogged across the cracked asphalt, the wind had picked up and was blowing all sorts of debris and twigs around the abandoned base.

Way off to their left was a number of aircraft shelters. Spire had read that they were so tough that the only way to demolish them apparently would be to hit them directly with

111

a large bomb, which would also happen to wipe out the town of Woodbridge, so understandable, they had been left.

As they approached what Spire surmised to be the WSA or weapons storage area, he was surprised to see how huge it was. A set of buildings off to their right looked like it might have been some kind of security post. As they approached they could see that there were high, double fences running around the area, topped with two to three feet of twisted barbed wire, together with signs everywhere confirming that they were approaching a restricted area.

Beyond the fence were the storage bunkers that had once housed the nuclear weapons. "We can't access the site. Apart from it being restricted, the area is secure," Isobel said.

"It used to be restricted, but surely not now. Besides, I can already see a way in, we won't have to breach the perimeter fence," Spire said, having already located an area where the chain-link fence had been peeled back away from one of the concrete posts, allowing easy access to the WSA area beyond.

"Oh great, I was hoping you'd not notice that," Isobel replied, rolling her eyes.

"Come on, ten minutes and I promise we can go," Spire said, not really knowing what he was looking for, but also too curious to leave the base just yet.

As they both carefully squeezed through the gap in the fence, Spire thought back to their meeting with Trent and his confirmation of the UFO's beaming lights down to the WSA, as if they somehow had the ability to gather information from the bunkers or, even more startlingly, actually deactivate the weapons that were supposedly kept here.

They both rounded one of the sinister mounds, the tops of which were covered with grass, and found the front, a solid section of concrete with a solitary steel door set into the same. The door had three large dead bolts fitted to it which slid on steel runners into a three 'U' sections on the adjoining steel panel. Two of the bolts were buckled and had come away from the runners, but the middle one was still in position. Spire grabbed it and tried to pull it back, and was shocked to find it retracted.

"So much for security eh?" he said, as he pulled on the heavy door, which slowly creaked open.

"Unbelievable," Isobel muttered, looking around the desolate row of bunkers which formed the WSA.

As Spire opened the heavy door a damp, mouldy smell escaped. They both peered into the dark, cobweb-filled silo. Overhead they could see some type of pulley, which was no doubt used to carry the weapons into position. The floor appeared to be made of reinforced concrete, badly cracked in some places. At the far end of the bunker they could make out another vault-style steel door. The wind was picking up and now had a cold bite to it. "Let's have a very quick look and we'll get the hell out of here," Spire said.

Isobel rolled her eyes. "Very quick," she said, frowning.

Spire found a large rock and rolled it in front of the door, making sure it couldn't possibly lock even if it was blown shut again. He turned his torch on and they both headed inside, just as a cold drizzle started to fall.

The silo was made from panels of solid reinforced concrete. There were old wooden crates stacked up over on the left side, covered in huge cobwebs. Above them, fixed to the curved roof of the silo was a steel overhead gantry which extended the length of the structure and, was presumably used for moving the nuclear weapons into the silo and to their storage locations at the back, which Spire could see consisted of a wall of solid smooth steel cylindrical slots, or racking, much like a huge howitzer rack, with enough slots to store around 25 weapons.

As Spire and Isobel moved towards the structure to get a better look at it, they heard a loud metallic thud, which echoed around the confined space. Simultaneously, the silo was thrown into darkness. They both jumped as they heard the bang, followed by a faint *beep, beep, beeping* sound. They immediately turned, and as they did, their worst fears were realised – the silo door had been slammed shut, but not only that, there was an object on the ground, red LED lights glowing, and a counter ticking down.

CHAPTER 21

Great Falls
Washington, USA

DR ADRIAN RAYTON prepared for a meeting of his most trusted, and senior members of the *Weapons Industry Research* branch of the U.S. Department of Energy - DOE, a discreetly funded, special black projects team; a team which all had devoted their lives to for the sake of the *Aquarius Project.*

They would be arriving at his Great Falls home at 7.30 P.M, a little under an hour from now, to discuss the latest developments and analysis, and fallout from the assassination of Professor Lazarus a few weeks earlier in London.

Rayton stepped into the shower, after admiring himself in the bathroom mirror for a few moments. His hair was now grey, but at least he still had a full head of it, and although now in his mid-sixties, he still felt young and fit, which was something he needed to maintain if he was to oversee this clandestine, shadow government force for another decade, which he certainly intended to do. He'd seen out five U.S. Presidents so far and fully intended on seeing out the most recently elected President too, and judging by his age, that shouldn't be a problem. He smiled as he stood under the hot shower. Little wonder that the President of the United States isn't vested with the necessary security clearance on what the DOE really does, deep within its vast compartmentalised estate. Each President of the United States is only empowered for eight years; not nearly long enough to appreciate the sensitive knowledge required for monitoring and maintaining what really goes on here. It would be pointless, and dangerous.

Ever since it had been decided by the powers that be, following the 1947 crash, to create a powerful, shadow government which doesn't need to answer or report to the legislative branches of the elected government. The shadow government had been allowed to create its own functional branches, in order to research and develop exotic technologies and advanced weapons, to ensure the safety of the United States, allowing it to maintain global superiority and of course to carry out special operations, using specialised and highly mobile, elite military units who answered to nobody. Yes, it had been a thrilling forty-five years heading up one of the most powerful clandestine units on the planet.

Professor Lazarus had been removed from the picture; he'd gone too far with his public presentation. Decades ago when he'd spoken out about exotic technology and captured 'alien' discs over at Area 51, the department had agonised over what to do about the leak, but a novel idea had been proposed. Instead of reacting and trying to cover things up, much like the earlier efforts of Project Blue Book and many other debunking strategies, they'd decided to just leave Lazarus. Let him speak about what he'd seen – nobody would believe him anyway.

That strategy had worked, until recently. But, this time he'd gone too far. He had to be taken care of. The Department would have taken care of him, but a surprising development had arisen, and it had been agreed for the Catholic Church, in view of their fear of disclosure, to deal with the problem instead. The solution had been perfect, but now there were even more loose ends, and they needed taking care of too, hence the emergency meeting being called today.

Rayton stepped out of the shower and towelled himself dry; he shaved, walked into his spacious bedroom, and pulled out a grey linen shirt from the extensive collection in his

116

wardrobe. He dressed casually, but smartly, and went downstairs to his lounge to wait for the rest of the team to arrive. He poured himself some bourbon, topped it up with a measure of water, and relaxed into his soft brown leather sofa.

Pride of place, above his fireplace, was a seventy by seventy-inch print of the plains of St Augusta, near Roswell, in New Mexico. He loved the picture. Each time he looked at the dry, arid, desert plain, he was reminded of the impact site of the craft that changed everything; a craft that had travelled the gulf of space, tens of light years, before disaster had struck and caused it to crash. It was of course no coincidence the thing crashed within a hop and a skip from the Trinity atom bomb test site. Splitting the atom had caused unparalleled external interest with what mankind had achieved a few years' earlier at that particular location.

The rest of the comfortable room was decorated tastefully with a cream carpet, a set of mahogany book shelves, full of novels and technical science books on quantum physics and space. A couple of large pots filled with ferns and yucca plants added some greenery. On the floor, positioned looking out and up towards the heavens, was a four-foot high statue of the Italian Astronomer and physicist, Galileo Galilei.

Rayton appreciated Galileo as the genius that he was. A man ahead of his time, whose study of speed and velocity, gravity, inertia and relativity gave mankind so much, not to mention his observations of the celestial bodies of the Solar System. Yes, Galileo would be honoured to have had one of humankind's most adventurous and scientific projects named after him. In front of Galileo were two sets of double French doors, which opened up onto three acres of rear south facing garden, which were illuminated by rows of solar lighting once the sun went down.

Rayton's cell phone suddenly beeped, telling him there was a vehicle approaching along his main driveway, sensors triggering the signal to his cell phone.

He took one last look out towards his grounds, gave the Galileo statue an affectionate pat on the head, and headed for the main door to greet his guests.

CHAPTER 22

RAF Woodbridge

SPIRE AND ISOBEL sprinted over to the steel door, which appeared to have been deliberately closed and locked. *Jeez, this can't be happening?* Spire said to himself, as he reached the door.

As he ran for the door he shouted to Isobel. "Find out what the hell that thing beeping is and do something about it!"

Isobel knelt down and looked at the black cylindrical device on the ground. A red, LED timer displayed 9:52 and was counting down. She rolled the cylinder over to check for any decals, or any clue as to what it might be. She found some;

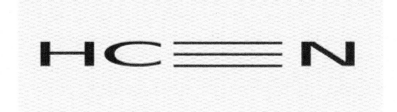

She stared at the symbols for a few seconds before recognising them.

As Spire gave up trying to manually wrench open the door, he looked down at Isobel. "Give me the bad news," he said.

She looked up, tears rolling down her cheeks. "It's bad, very bad. It's a canister of hydrogen cyanide."

"*Jesus.* We need to find a way to get out, and fast. Quickly, grab those hessian sacks and pile them up over here," he shouted, as he ran back to the locked door. "*Hello, hello?*" he screamed. "Open the God-damn door!" He placed his ear against the door, but he couldn't hear anything. He took a few steps back and ran at it, ramming it with his shoulder, but he just slammed into the thick steel door, jarring his upper arm.

"What are we going to do? I knew we should never have come in here," Isobel said, her voice barely audible, her emotions bubbling over.

"Calm down. Let me think. I'll get us out of here, I promise," Spire said, trying to relax her. He removed his cell phone, but as expected, there was no signal inside the reinforced bomb proof weapons storage bunker. Isobel checked her phone, but the battery was dead.

With no seemingly way out of the silo, and the canister's LCD counter ticking down, Spire shone his light towards the numerous crates that were stacked up on the left hand side of the bunker. He walked over to them and started removing the lids to see if there was anything of use inside them. Large spiders scurried everywhere, but after checking on the final crate, he found nothing. He moved further along the left hand side of the confined space, Isobel sticking closely by his side. The weapons storage slots were of course empty, the nuclear missiles that were allegedly once stored there, long ago relocated. There was a dark space to the right of the slots where the racking didn't quite fit snuggly up against the right side of the rising arched wall, and some kind of vault with a submarine-style door lock. The beam of his torch then washed over something shiny. Spire bent down and could see it was a wrench. "This might help," he said to Isobel, grabbing it. Spire then tried to twist the vault door lock, but it was stuck, or jammed solid. "*God damn it,*" he shouted.

They both ran back to the front of the silo and Spire immediately set to work, ramming the thin end of the wrench into the edge of the door, where there was a tiny gap between the crumbling concrete wall and the door fitting. Isobel shone the torch onto the spot, as he did his best to get some purchase on the wrench to try and leverage the door open, but after ninety long seconds of trying, he realised his efforts were useless. He cursed again, trying not to sound too stressed, so as not to upset Isobel.

Spire threw the wrench to the floor and looked up to the overhead gantry, and as he did, an idea came to him. "Quick, help me stack some of these crates up," he said.

He and Isobel then dragged six of the crates to the centre of the silo, enough for Spire to stand on in order to reach the hook which was dangling down from a steel cable, part of the overhead gantry.

The rusty steel cable started to slowly unwind, squeaking and creaking as he pulled it down towards him. A pang of excitement washed over him as he realised he might be able to somehow connect it up to the door, allowing him to yank the door off its hinges. As he pulled it the twenty-feet or so distance towards the door, the cable abruptly jerked to a stop, seemingly jammed. Spire pulled on it again as hard as he could, Isobel joining him, but the thing was stuck. "*Shit!*" Spire shouted, starting to feel somewhat helpless.

Isobel caught her breath. "I didn't want to tell you, but I don't know if you noticed, the motor for the cable mechanism appears to have been removed anyway. We're screwed," she said.

Spire didn't want to admit he'd not noticed that crucial aspect. He slumped onto one of the crates, the LCD timer counting down past 7:45. Things didn't look good, *but there had to be some way out,* he reasoned.

CHAPTER 23

Great Falls
Washington, USA

RAYTON HEARD A car engine outside and glanced out of the window that overlooked the front driveway, and saw a black Buick pull up.

A minute or so later, he opened the door to his four colleagues; two of them, males, were well-built and athletic in appearance, short crew cuts, one fair, one dark and both wearing jeans, T-shirts and leather jackets. The other male was much slimmer, intellectual type and dressed casually in slacks and a cotton jacket. The solitary female was well presented, her hair pulled back, very business-like with clinical features, a pale complexion and she wore no makeup.

"Welcome," Rayton said, gesturing them all in. "Come, we'll go straight down to the Op's Room."

The men nodded and followed Rayton along a corridor which took them past the lounge, along the back of the house, and down a set of carpeted stairs to a secure sub-level door. Rayton placed his palm onto an entry pad fixed to the wall, which glowed blue momentarily, before a steel door slid open with a hydraulic whine.

The guests followed him in.

The secure basement room had been built one level under the ground; with two-foot thick reinforced concrete walls, floor and roof. The thirty foot by twenty foot room had white panelling; the floor was carpeted in a luxurious cream carpet. A rectangular two-inch thick smoked glass table sat in the middle of the room, surrounded by eight brown leather high-backed chairs.

Arranged on the table, in front of six of the seats, were pencil-thin computer slots to allow monitors to rise up from discreet housings under the table. Two much larger monitors were fixed on the end wall, one displaying a real time image of the globe, the North and South American continent, which was about to descend into darkness. The other displayed a view of the Northern Hemisphere, live images from a DOE geostationary global surveyor satellite, orbiting some 20,000 miles above the Earth. Along each wall were framed pictures of some of the great astronomers and physicists, Copernicus, Galileo, and Sir Isaac Newton.

"Take a seat, my friends," Rayton said. "Can I get any of you a drink, before we start? I'm having another bourbon."

"That sounds good, I'll have the same," the slender man in the cream cotton jacket, wearing round wire-rimmed glasses, said.

"A beer would be good," the blonde man said.

The other guy nodded. "Same," he said.

"And you, Sparrow, what would you like?"

"Something cold, non-alcoholic, would be fine, their female colleague said."

"Very well, give me a moment," Rayton said, leaving them briefly before returning with a tray of drinks and handing them out. The visitors appeared serious, but calm, as they all held their drinks up and clinked glasses.

"So, the purpose of this meeting is to discuss the present situation following the necessary elimination of Lazarus in the U.K., and the current events on the ground there, which are unfolding as I speak," Rayton said, sipping his drink.

"We didn't expect Lazarus' removal to be so problematic. Perhaps we should have left him alone, come up with some embarrassing, fake revelations about him to counter the damage he was about to do instead?" Sparrow suggested.

There was a short silence. "We did discuss the options thoroughly before arriving at our decision. The fact the necessary action was carried out by the Vatican was a surprise, but it seemed like the perfect solution at the time," Rayton replied.

"Quite," Sparrow responded.

"We will discuss that issue shortly. As for now, we have two agents on the ground in Rendlesham, Suffolk, where the Englishman, Spire, and his Russian friend, are snooping around. They both appear to be onto something and so I decided it best if they were dealt with swiftly before they discovered anything useful. Hawk and Condor are taking care of things for us over there," Rayton added.

"What about the other attendees, no indication that any others took Lazarus' presentation seriously?" the dark haired man, whose codename was Eagle, asked.

"Not at present, but all our electronic resources are being brought to bear to monitor the position. Appropriate and proportionate action will be taken if necessary," Rayton said, taking another sip of bourbon.

"And what of the upcoming intelligence community report in the Covid Relief Bill that our last President, in his wisdom, decided to sign?" Owl asked, adjusting his glasses.

Rayton raised his eyes from the table. The team could see he looked troubled. "We will do our best to limit the damage, but it won't be easy. There will be some intriguing disclosure of some inexplicable events within the report, no doubt, but with a bit of spin in the right places, we should be able to limit the fallout."

"We've had to ridicule witnesses and add the right mix of smoke and mirrors to previous events in order to limit their impact. We have come a long way since the Roswell debacle," Sparrow said, looking at the men from over her spectacles.

Eagle placed his beer down on the table. "Don't forget the DOE almost screwed up big time with the Dayton, Texas incident, back in 1980. Pure luck got us off the hook there."

There was a moment's silence. "If you're referring to the Cash-Landrum sighting, named after the two unfortunate witnesses who just happened to be in the wrong place at the wrong time, which resulted in them being exposed to ionising radiation, you're correct. Retro-fitting a downed E.T. craft with a nuclear reactor and plasma centrifuge was always going to end in disaster. That said, had the graphite housing not failed, the test flight would have been successful," Sparrow responded, somewhat defending the DOE's position.

"No risk, no reward, eh?" Eagle said.

"Come on folks, we're not here to discuss historical operations, but to resolve current ones," Rayton intervened.

Sparrow shrugged off Eagle's comment.

"Okay Gentlemen, and Sparrow, please take a look at the monitors in front of you," Rayton said.

The four of them diverted their gaze down to the monitors rising from the table, glowing white as the screens lit up as they rose.

"What you see on your screens are live images from Rendlesham in the U.K. Apollo Team, Hawk and Condor are just taking care of the loose ends I mentioned at the start of the meeting. I thought you'd enjoy seeing the events as they unfold in real time, together with a brief view of the airbase as it now is," Rayton said.

The guests looked at their screens with renewed interest as the images from the DOE's Keyhole Class, *Silent Star* spy satellite, orbiting 125 miles above the Earth, were beamed down. Grainy images, getting clearer by the second revealed their agents moving across the ground in Suffolk, U.K.

CHAPTER 24

RAF Woodbridge

HAWK AND CONDOR had just finished locking their targets in the silo, when they reported back to the rest of the team, who they knew were now looking in on their mission from the Op's Room. Hawk even looked up to the sky and gave an arrogant wink, knowing the DOE's; *Silent Star* was able to see him.

As they both moved across the open ground towards the hole in the security fence, Hawk thought he caught glimpse of something black move behind the concrete storage building two-hundred feet distant.

"Did you see that?" he asked Condor, as they moved swiftly through the small breach in the weapons storage fence and on towards the main perimeter fence where they'd entered the base.

"Was it a bird?" Hawk responded, looking towards the concrete block.

They continued moving along the main fence, both men glancing towards the concrete storage block as they did. The wind had continued to pick up and dark clouds were now rolling in from the Atlantic, casting dark shadows over the desolate base. Both men were reassured that the DOE spy satellite was keeping an eye on them a hundred plus miles above. Rayton would alert them to any danger, if there was any.

Inside the concrete structure a figure stood, motionless, his black thermal clothing, the latest state-of-the-art, military satellite camouflage equipment he'd acquired from his old contacts, shielded him from any thermal imaging scopes and most prying satellites. He waited; his Desert Eagle strapped firmly to his Kevlar body shield, well hidden under the thermal masking equipment he was wearing.

Hawk and Condor were now opposite the storage building, the hole in the perimeter fence just forty feet further along from their position.

Suddenly, a *thud,* from over to their left, emanating from near the concrete storage building, caught their attention. They both froze and looked in the direction of the dilapidated building. As they did, they saw a small rock, or stone, seemingly fly out from behind the building, or was it the entrance? They couldn't quite tell.

"What the fuck?" Condor whispered to Hawk.

"Apollo Team to base. Do you have us in your sights," Hawk whispered into his mic.

There was a few seconds pause, before Rayton's familiar voice responded. "We do, *Silent Star* is watching you as we speak."

"Can you see anything unusual?" Hawk asked.

"Negative, nothing unusual showing up in your immediate vicinity," Rayton's reassuring voice confirmed.

Hawk nodded and signalled for Condor to go take a closer look.

Condor pulled out his hunting knife and crept over to the concrete building, moving silently, his back now up against the crumbling wall with the faded A-10 *Tankbuster* Muriel. With his knife drawn, he edged along the building towards the entrance. Hawk looked on from the perimeter fence, thirty feet away.

Condor reached the end of the wall and listened. He heard nothing. *Perhaps the deserted base was just giving them the jitters?* He signalled to Hawk that everything appeared okay, and proceeded around the corner, knife drawn, sliding along the wall to the building's entrance. He waited and listened for a few seconds, before proceeding inside.

He wasn't prepared for what happened next. As soon as he stepped into the building, he immediately detected a blur of motion, something black above him. He then felt a powerful forearm grab him around the neck, and before he could react and use his knife on his attacker, he felt, and heard his neck *crack*.

The man flexed his biceps as he lowered the limp body to the ground, before bending down and frisking the dead man. He found a wallet, and pulled it out, just as he heard the other target approach the building. The dark figure quickly pocketed the dead man's wallet, just as a voice erupted over some static from the deceased man's radio.

"Condor, what's going on? What is your status?"

The dark figure felt his heart beat faster. He only had seconds, but he had an idea.

CHAPTER 25

HAWK TRIED TO raise Condor on his communications device, but he got no response. Concerned, he drew his knife and ran over to the building, edged along to the entrance and craned his neck around and into the dark space. Hawk was confused at what he saw. Condor appeared to be seated atop a crate, his back to the entrance, and leaning forward onto the crate in front of him.

"Condor...Condor, are you alright man?"

There was no response. "Apollo Team to base. Are you getting this? Something odd. Condor is inside storage building near to the perimeter fence - immobile. Something is wrong. Respond."

Rayton's voice erupted from the small ear piece he was wearing. "We just picked up some erratic movement from inside the building, but we can only see you and Hawk on the high-res thermal imaging cameras. Use maximum caution," he said.

Hawk was feeling nervous for the first time in a long while. Something was definitely wrong. He proceeded inside. "Buddy, what the hell you doing?" he said, as he extended his arm and placed it on Condor's shoulder. As soon as he touched him, his colleagues' lifeless body slumped to the ground.

Hawk spun around to check if anyone or anything was behind him, but the crumbling building was empty, just a few crates, hessian sacks and an old black tarpaulin on the ground, close to where he was standing. Hawk nervously stooped down and felt Condor's neck for a pulse, there wasn't one.

As he was about to stand up and report back to command, the black tarpaulin over to his left erupted from the ground, and a tall, dark figure seemingly sprung up from nowhere.

Hawk then realised that there was some kind of drainage channel cut into the concrete, where the tarpaulin had been, the channel large enough for a man, a muscular man, to lay down in.

Hawk twisted around, still in shock, but managed to bring his knife down on the figure. The hunting knife made contact with the man's chest, but it stopped dead, like it had struck a brick wall. Hawk realised the man was wearing some kind of body armour. All sorts of things started flashing through his mind. *Why hadn't Rayton seen this coming? Who was this person? How could he and Condor have been caught out like this?*

The thoughts whirled around his mind, as he felt a sharp pain in his back, near the spinal column, and then a *crack*, a bone breaking. *Was that my neck?* he wondered, as he fell onto the ground next to his friend, before everything turned to permanent darkness.

Breathing heavily, the man frisked the dead military-man, found his wallet, and pocketed it. He then exiting the building and sprinted for the WSA perimeter fence, squeezed through the hole and ran on towards the weapons silo.

CHAPTER 26

THE RED, LCD lights on the cyanide canister ticked passed 48 seconds. Spire and Isobel had grabbed the few hessian sacks they'd found at the back of the silo and placed the canister inside one of them, and had then placed it inside one of the nuclear weapons racks, using the remaining two sacks to plug the individual weapons slot as best they could. Spire knew the effort to prevent the cyanide or whatever was inside the canister coming out was a futile one. All they'd done was create an elaborate and deadly firework.

He and Isobel were now crouched down close to the silo's steel door, waiting for the inevitable to happen. Spire had run out of ideas. He'd always managed to find a way of getting out of difficult situations, but his luck had appeared to have run out this time. He'd taken his eye off the ball, not seen or appreciated the danger they were in.

"I know people say their lives flash in front of them when they know they are going to die," Isobel said. "But all I can think about is the life I will miss in the future. I wanted a daughter, or a son to enjoy the rest of my life with. That's what I am thinking about right now."

Spire felt his emotions brimming over. He felt guilty for getting Isobel involved in this mission, and he cursed himself for speaking to her at Lazarus' presentation, and for coming down here. It wasn't even part of the mission he'd been given. Oliver hadn't even asked him to come down to Rendlesham. He started thinking about Angela. He never expected to be joining her so soon, but he should have known with his line of work it was likely to be sooner, rather than later.

"I'm so sorry," he said, squeezing Isobel's hand.

She didn't respond. A hissing sound at the far end of the room had caught her attention.

Spire felt his stomach turn over as he realised what it was – cyanide gas escaping from the canister.

"You know what this will do to us right?" Isobel said, matter-of-factly, her Russian accent heavy.

Spire remained silent, suspecting she was about to tell him anyway.

"If left untreated, we will develop acute headache, drowsiness, nausea and vomiting. Then convulsions, a slow, irregular heart rate, blue lips, followed coma and then, death."

"Oh and there's me thinking it would be bad," Spire replied, flippantly.

As they sat there, with the canister hissing, a visible white / yellow mist started creeping over the floor towards them. It looked like the bad special effects from a 1960's horror movie, except this was no graveyard, and they weren't vampires, but they would soon be dead, Spire realised.

As the mist started to envelop them both, Spire hugged Isobel for the last time, his thoughts wandering to Angela, his cat Charlie and Kim. He drew shallow breaths, not wanting to take in any of the killer gas, Isobel did the same.

Then, above the hissing sound came another much louder, *clinking* noise. *Was the thing going to explode too?*

Suddenly the silo erupted with light, natural, bright light, and a rush of fresh air, as they both fell backwards, and out onto the concrete pad just outside the silo entrance.

As Spire covered his eyes to protect them from the sudden light, trying to grasp what had just happened, he saw a dark figure hunched over him.

"God-damn it Rob, you sure as hell scared the shit out of me. I thought you'd smoked your last cigar pal," the voice boomed.

Spire rolled over and sat cross-legged on the concrete pad. "I don't believe it. Is that you Travis?" he said, his eyes adjusting to the external light, and his friend's unmistakable hulking figure, chiselled jaw and cropped dark hair.

"I'm still feeling a little jet-lagged from the flight over, but adrenalin is now well and truly flowing forcefully through my veins," Dexter said, helping Spire and Isobel off the floor.

Spire and Isobel just looked at him, clearly still in shock.

"I had an odd feeling after speaking to you on the phone a few days back. Perhaps a sixth sense was subtly operating, I don't know, but now I'm damn glad I listened to it. I just felt you were in trouble. If I'd not have followed you down to Suffolk as soon I landed at Heathrow, you'd both be dead.

Spire shook his head. "What happened? Who locked us in here?" he asked.

"I arrived on the base just in time to see the two military-looking types lock you both in the missile silo. I knew they couldn't be military however, but something more sinister. I waited for them both at the storage building and dealt with them." Dexter said.

"Dealt with them?" Isobel spoke for the first time.

"Yes ma'am. They won't be bothering either of you again, but no doubt whoever is responsible, will send others. Clearly someone or some organisation is very concerned you're snooping around down here," Dexter said. "It's a miracle you're both still alive. I almost didn't get here. I was slowed down by a terrible accident back on the main road. A red pick-up had ploughed into a tractor, flipped over, landing upside down in a field," he added, stepping back from the white mist now escaping from the silo.

"Hydrogen cyanide," Isobel spluttered as she rubbed and shielded her eyes from the wind and light.

"Very unpleasant; come on; let's get the hell off the base. We're not safe here," Dexter said.

"A red pick-up? You're kidding. That was what Trent was driving," he said, looking at Isobel, who already had a look of despair spreading over her face.

"It was a mess. I would have arrived earlier, but the black Bronco was close to the accident scene, I just followed it all the way to the base here, saw the two military guys get out, figured straight away something wasn't right."

Spire looked at his friend and shook his head. "We met with a witness before we came here. He was driving a red pick-up. Those sons-of-bitches must have been responsible for his accident," Spire said.

Dexter shook his head. "I spoke with the cop re-routing the traffic. He told me they'd been a fatality. I'm sorry if it was your contact," he said.

Spire shook his head in despair, but put a brave face on for Dexter. "I can't believe you travelled all the way over and followed us down here. Thank God you did, as my nine lives were about to well and truly expire," Spire said, glancing at Isobel.

A sudden, loud fluttering from above caught their attention, and the three of them looked skywards. A flock of birds must have been disturbed from the trees surrounding the base and were flying overhead.

"I don't like this, come on, let's go, now!" Dexter said, as the three of them set off jogging towards the WSA perimeter fence.

CHAPTER 27

Great Falls
Washington, USA

THE TEAM STUDIED the faces of the three individuals looking up at them, *Silent Star* beaming back a perfect image of them from 125 miles up.

"Could this get any worse?" Eagle said, shaking his head in disbelief. "I mean we have two of our supposed best agents on the ground there and this son-of-a-bitch manages to despatch them both, with considerable ease I might add."

Nobody said a thing. They were all still transfixed to the still image of the three individuals looking skywards.

"We know Spire and the Russian of course, but an Identity check is being run as we speak on their mystery guardian angel," Rayton said, his voice serious and sombre.

"Who's going to clean the mess up over there?" Sparrow snapped.

"We have some assets within two hundred miles of the location. They will be tasked to go in and clean up," Rayton replied, tapping away on a keyboard in front of him.

"I admit, we seriously underestimated Robert Spire's contacts," Rayton said, as he read the data now streaming down his screen, obtained from multiple DOE sources and assets. "We appear to be dealing with one, Travis Dexter, an ex-marine who served with the United States Army in two tours of duty, Gulf War One and, most recently, Afghanistan. Multiple enemy kills, exceedingly fearless, very tough and versatile by the looks of things. For the last ten years or so he has been undertaking private security work, but he isn't just a killer to hire. Seems like he has some moral compass too, which in a way makes him more determined and dangerous. He is clearly a force to be reckoned with," he said, looking up from the screen.

The team remained silent.

"Eagle, I want you to track this Dexter character, Spire and the girl down, and eliminate them. Take with you whatever agents you feel you'll need as these three could cause us problems further down the road."

The dark-haired man looked around the room with his deep, inset, reptilian-looking eyes, then back at Rayton. "With pleasure; I will finish off the job Hawk and Condor clearly weren't up to completing," he said, taking a final gulp of beer.

"Very good," Rayton replied.

"And what about the any other loose ends we might have?" Sparrow asked.

"Well, we all know our friend from Quell-Tech Labs has been monitoring things, for his and his paymasters own legitimate reasons. We can just about trust Sentenza. We are, after all, on the same side here. Maintaining secrecy, preserving the status quo and of course, ensuring that the U.S Dollar remains the dominant currency, the Petro-Dollar system, remains intact and that current aviation and rocket technology is kept in place. The longer we keep our exotic technologies under wraps, the better it is for everyone," Rayton said.

"So, it's business as usual then?" Owl replied after a few seconds.

"Yes, business as usual, apart from one additional loose end we should really take care of."

"And what is that?" Owl asked.

"The Vatican connection," Rayton said.

"You're not suggesting we take out the Pope?!"

"Not the Pope, no, but I am concerned about the three scholars that Lazarus went to see. They ordered the kill on Lazarus, which did us a favour. Sentenza has helped us by taking out the assassin. Our friends Condor and Hawk were at least able to verify that for us, but what we don't want is for there to be any more leaks about this. My concern is that one or more of them might talk about what Lazarus revealed to them."

"What do you propose?" Sparrow asked.

"I propose that you take ownership of this problem. Use whatever resources you require, but ensure that the potential problem is...eliminated," Rayton said, smiling.

Sparrow nodded. "Yes sir."

Rayton got up from his chair and slowly walked around the table. "The time is right to show you all something," he said, walked to the end of the room and over to the large framed *Galileo* picture. He admired it for a while, before reaching out and pressing a concealed button in the picture frame. The entire frame slid to the left, revealing a steel vault embedded in the wall.

Rayton tapped a code into the vault's alpha-numeric keypad, and the enclosed room resonated with the sound of three large steel bolts retracting within the vault's steel door.

Rayton pulled the vault door open and reached in and took out two, faded, manila envelopes and carefully extracted the documents that were inside. Grainy, black and white photographs, before turning and heading back over to the table.

The four team members were all looking at the envelopes and the photographs, eager to see what they might be. On the first envelope, written in black type below the words *MAGIC / USAP EYES ONLY*;

LUNAR OTBITER 1; MOSAIC – MOON 1966.

On the second envelope was written;

SHAG HARBOUR: CRASHED DISC -1967

Rayton placed the black and white photographs on the table in front of the group. "You are looking at part of the mosaic of images sent back by the Lunar 1 Orbiter, taken by the spacecraft as it passed over the far, or dark side of the Moon back in 1966, when NASA was surveying our closest satellite for a suitable landing spot for the Apollo missions."

The four of them stared at the ten inch by seven-inch glossy photographs, their eyes widening in disbelief.

"What the hell is that?" Sparrow finally asked, her expression revealing a mix of wonder and fear.

Owl turned one of the pictures so he could see it from a better angle. The photograph showed clear images of concentric, and other artificial-looking structures. "This shows the surface of the Moon. Are they genuine?" he asked, nervously.

Rayton looked at his guests, and then back down at the photographs. "Well, put it this way, we didn't build it," he said, lowering his voice.

A few seconds passed, nobody said a word.

Rayton then placed the solitary photograph he'd removed from the other envelope down on the table.

"This image was taken was taken at a depth of 158 feet at the bottom of *Shag Harbour,* off the coast of Nova Scotia. The object remains there to this day, as it was considered too high risk to retrieve."

The group looked at each other in stunned silence, and then up at Rayton.

"Anyway, lady and gentlemen, this meeting is over. These are the secrets we must protect. You have your tasks. See that they are completed. We will meet again in a few weeks to see where we are."

The team around the table dragged their eyes from the photographs in front of them, and looked at him, fear and wonder in their eyes.

"Godspeed to each of you," Rayton said to the group, as the monitors slid back into the table, and he gathered the photographs up and briskly placed them back into the manila envelope.

CHAPTER 28

SPIRE, DEXTER AND Isobel made it back to Spire's Range Rover. Exhausted and cold, Spire helped Isobel into the passenger seat. "I really can't thank you enough, Travis," he said to his friend, as he closed the door.

"No need for that Rob. I'm damn glad I listened to my instincts."

"You and I both," Spire said, as he headed over to the driver's side, reached in with the ignition fob and pressed the engine start button, turning the Rover's engine over to make sure it hadn't been sabotaged. "Listen, where you parked? I'll run you to your vehicle in case those knuckle heads have done something to it."

"Good point. I'm a few hundred feet back along the road," Dexter said, jumping in the back.

Spire carefully reversed out of the bushes and back onto the main road, and accelerated further along towards a black Ford he could see parked on the verge.

"So how in the hell did you manage to stay unseen?" Spire asked.

"Did you notice the unusual quality of the gear I'm wearing?" Dexter said, from the back.

"Well, apart from it being all black and padded, it did look a little...glittery," Spire replied.

"The glitter, as you refer to it, is actually a top secret, patented technology, which allows for maximum dexterity, combined with maximum body-heat blocking capability, making it virtually undetectable from any form of heat-seeking equipment, including satellites."

Isobel turned around. "That's very cool. I'm sure you didn't get that in Saville Row?" she smiled.

Dexter laughed. "It's very difficult to survive without a technological edge. I knew I'd need something like this to give myself a chance," he said, as he pulled out from his pocket the two dead men's wallets he'd taken.

"Well thank God it worked," Isobel said.

Dexter rifled through the Wallets. He found a standard U.S. driving license in each of them. One belonged to a Mr Ben Stulman, with an Ohio address; the other a Mr Richard Sterner, Arizona. No doubt they were both false I.D's, but he'd check the names and addresses later to be sure. Apart from some U.S dollars and British notes in both wallets, they were empty. He was just about to pocket them again when he noticed the end of a white card stuck against the leather credit card pouch in Sterner's wallet. "What have we got here?" he muttered.

"Found something?" Spire asked, from the front, as he pulled up alongside Dexter's hire car.

"Maybe," Dexter said, studying the simple white card, which had the words;

Department of Energy

embossed on it in black lettering, together with the DOE's, 1000 Independence Avenue, Washington address. "Might be nothing, or it could be that one of those goons was very careless. I've found what looks like a business card belonging to the *Department of Energy*. Could be linked, something for us to look into further later," he said, getting out.

"So what's the plan now? You're staying in London somewhere I assume? I'll be heading into the centre to drop Isobel off, but I'll probably need to head home for a night or two before we head over to the States – on the assumption that's what GLENCOM wants us to do. You're welcome to stay a night or two down in Wales, but it's a fair drive from London," Spire said.

Dexter stooped down slightly to look through Spire's open window. "Are there any casinos down near you?" he asked, winking at Isobel.

Spire raised his eyebrows and was about to speak.

"Well that's mighty kind of you pal, but I'm not sure I fancy the extra trek down, besides, you'll be busy preparing for the mission I'm sure. Next time buddy. I'll follow you back into London and we can meet up when GLENCOM want us to move," he said, giving the roof of Spire's Range Rover a hefty slap.

"No problem, sounds good. Okay, well let's get going. I'll make sure I don't lose you," he said.

Dexter jumped into his vehicle and Spire pulled off, accelerating gently along the perimeter road, RAF Woodbridge getting slowly smaller in the rear view mirror as he drove away. "I really won't be heading back there in a hurry," he said, glancing at Isobel.

Isobel smiled. "That was too close for comfort, but if I had to die today, I'm glad it would have been with you."

Spire took in a deep breath, not really having a response to that. "Well today wasn't our day to die, but it sounds like we can't say the same for poor old Mr Trent.

CHAPTER 29

Two Days Later
Budapest

RABBI, NEIL GREGORIUS walked briskly along the banks of the Danube, passing one of his favourite restaurants, Gundel, although unfortunately he had no time to eat there today, and neither did he have much of an appetite. Over to his left, the dark waters of the river flowed by. He knew he shouldn't really be venturing out, Bishop Valente had warned him, but he'd felt restless spending the last two weeks at home, and besides, he needed some exercise otherwise he'd completely seize up.

Over to the west, the fortified walls of Buda Castle rose up from Castle Hill, and ahead, further along the banks of the Danube he could see the majestic spires of the parliament building.

He walked by one of Budapest's many bridges – the Liberty Bridge, that spans the Danube and glanced momentarily at a pair of young lovers, kissing as they tossed a key to the padlock they'd just shackled to the bridge's ironwork, into the Danube, an age-old tradition in the city. Gregorius continued on, suddenly having the odd feeling that somebody might be following him.

The mid-afternoon sun was low in the sky, leaving long shadows on the surface of the fast moving river and on the imposing stone buildings that flanked the banks in this part of the city.

Rabbi Gregorius stopped briefly by a tree to catch his breath, suddenly feeling a little panicked. He mopped his forehead, certain someone had been following him, but there was no sign of anyone close by on the foot path that ran alongside the river. His heart was beating faster than it should be. He knew he wasn't that fit, but still, it felt as if it were about to jump out of his chest.

He knew the knowledge he and the other two scholars had was a threat to all of their safety. Being part of this thing scared the hell out of him, but there was no turning back the clock. He was nervous and concerned for his safety, both factors no doubt causing his pulse to race.

He took a few deep breaths to try and calm down, before continuing toward the river bank. Eighty feet further was the *Elizabeth Bridge*, which spans the narrowest part of the river. It was still some 290 metres long however and he needed to cross it in order to reach home.

As he turned onto the bridge, he noted a lone figure hunched over the railings, staring down into the river. The bridge would normally be busy, with three traffic lanes in both directions, but because of some works going on, the bridge was currently closed to traffic. Gregorius hesitated, thinking the figure looked a little odd, but the person took no notice of him, so the rabbi continued walking. As he reached the centre of the bridge, where the lone figure was positioned, a voice startled him.

"Rabbi Gregorius?"

The rabbi stopped and looked towards the dark figure, somewhat startled, wondering if he might know the man.

"Yes, do I know you young man?" Gregorius asked, nervously.

The man slowly turned and shook his head. "No I don't think you do. I have been attending your synagogue however and wanted to let you know how much your prayers have helped me recently," the stranger said.

Gregorius was slightly taken aback, but suddenly felt a little more at ease. A fellow Jew who he may have helped with his prayers was always a good thing.

"I just wanted to personally thank you for the help you have given me," the man said, extending his arm to shake the rabbi's hand.

Rabbi Gregorius stepped closer and went to shake the man's hand. "Bless you, but I must be getting back," he said, as the stranger gripped his hand, somewhat tighter than was comfortable.

It was then that Gregorius noticed the stranger had been leaning on a coiled up length of rope, with a noose at the end of it. Suddenly, Gregorius felt himself being yanked forwards by the stranger, and before he knew what was going on, the stranger had placed the noose end of the rope around his neck.

"Please, no, what have I done wrong? What are you doing?"

"I'm sorry rabbi, but I'm afraid you know too much about things that never should have been disclosed to you," the stranger said.

"But...but, I have said nothing. We will not say anything. Please, you don't need to do this. I can help you, help you to change your mind, just give me a chance."

"I'm sorry rabbi, but I have my orders. Your God is all that can help you now," the man said, as he lifted the rabbi up and threw him over the railing and off the bridge. The man had made sure the rope wasn't sufficiently long enough to allow the rabbi to hit the water however, just in case he didn't drown.

Rabbi Gregorius felt weightless for a split second, a feeling of flying, like in the many dreams he'd had as a child, and then, a terrible *crack*, as his neck snapped.

The DOE agent hurried off the bridge and jogged to the nearest tram, quickly hopping on it, before heading to the airport to await further orders.

CHAPTER 30

Oakdale, Wales

ROBERT SPIRE PULLED into the rear car park belonging to his law office, and parked up. He entered via the back door, noting the alarm had been deactivated. It was just after 10 a.m. after all, and he could hear Kim typing away as he headed upstairs.

"Morning, stranger. Welcome back. I was beginning to wonder if a UFO might have zapped you up," Kim said, looking up from her computer screen as he walked in.

"Very funny, Kim; I did have a slight scare in Rendlesham Forest, and almost didn't get off the RAF base, but you can't get rid of me that easily," Spire said, smiling.

"Ooh really, tell me what happened?" Kim asked, suddenly a little more serious.

Spire told her what happened down in Suffolk, from the kids startling them in the forest with the remote controlled UFO, to the sudden escalation and serious situation he and Isobel found themselves in at RAF Woodbridge.

"Jesus Robert, I'm being serious when I say this, you really need to think about retiring from GLENCOM. It really isn't good for your health. It's a damn good job Travis turned up, clearly," she said, getting up to put the kettle on.

"I won't say no to a mug of fresh coffee help," Spire said, heading into his office.

"On its way boss," Kim shouted from the kitchen.

He sat down at his desk, stared briefly at the mound of letters in front of him, and swivelled his chair to face the wall-mounted plasma TV. He turned it on to catch up with the morning's news. The Russia / Ukraine issue was again grabbing the headlines. Russia had decided to amass a sizable number of troops and tanks close to the Ukraine border. The United States had slapped more sanctions on Russia and tensions were starting to simmer. Spire shook his head in despair; a real feeling of cold war tension seemed to be returning. It was a timely reminder that perhaps the old, dilapidated twin air bases of RAF Woodbridge and Bentwaters perhaps weren't as obsolete as they looked. Spire hoped all parties would see reason and tensions would cool as quickly as they had risen.

Spire flicked over to CNN, and a developing story immediately caught his attention. It was related to a U.S. Navy training exercise off the coast of California back in July 2019. The story had only just surfaced, according to the news anchor, but photographs and video footage taken by Navy personnel from the U.S. warships showed up to six flying craft of unknown origin, which couldn't be identified. The news anchor confirmed;

"US Navy warships were purportedly swarmed by up to six airborne objects, which performed brazen manoeuvres over the warships and close to a sensitive military training range. None of the warships, it seems, were able to identify the drones, if that's what they were, and the incident has baffled witnesses. According to one source, the U.S. Navy has evidence of the UFO's doing things that defy explanation, such as breaking the sound barrier without a sonic boom and performing flight characteristics, such as trans-medium capability – flying from air into water – which is considered impossible with current human technology. The question

148

on everyone's lips is, are they Russian, Chinese, or indeed, extra-terrestrial?"

The news anchor smiled at his colleague in the studio. *"I guess many people, including the Pentagon, are hoping the objects are actually extra-terrestrial, rather than the alternative!"* he said, smiling.

Kim walked in with two cups of coffee and sat down behind Spire's desk. "What's going on?" she asked.

"You're not going to believe it, but it was a report on U.S. warships being buzzed by UFO's back in 2019."

Kim glanced at the screen, just in time to catch the end of a replay showing earie, green, night-time footage of what appeared to be a pyramidal-shaped, bright object being filmed from the deck of one of the warships. "Good Lord, what the hell is that?"

"That's a good question. It's either foreign superpower technology, secret U.S. technology, or dare I say it, genuine UFO's," Spire said, sipping his coffee.

"Gee, Rob, this is crazy stuff. What's going on? Are the media and Pentagon trying to tell us something? Drip-feeding us UFO stuff in order to prepare us for some kind of announcement?" Kim asked.

Spire shrugged. "Beats me, but there's a hell of a lot of information coming out on the phenomenon," he said, as he went to turn the T.V. off.

"It's just weird," Kim said.

Spire flicked the channel to BBC News in error and a local news bulletin was being aired, the image of a country lane and police cordons, aerial footage of a tractor and a farmer's field, an upturned pickup resting there.

"A developing story down here involving a terrible accident, which seems to have resulted in the driver of the pickup colliding with a tractor at this normally quiet junction, and ending up in the farmer's field

across the road. Police are currently appealing for witnesses..."

Spire sighed, feeling terribly guilty about arranging to meet Trent. He turned the T.V. off. "Anyway, that's enough about UFO's for now, what's new in the world of law?" he asked Kim.

"Hmm, well I managed to finally settle the James case yesterday, the suggestion you made worked; One hundred and twenty-five thousand pounds. And, we have received a couple of new disease claims in this morning. I'll open the files, get the standard letters done, apply for the medical records and leave them on your desk for you to deal with."

"Great, well done on the James file, nice settlement. I know the poor bugger hasn't got long left, but at least he can enjoy the compensation."

The Mike James case had been running about two years. Spire's client, James - a storeroom worker at one of the local oil refineries - had been exposed to asbestos fibres back in the 1970's from old asbestos lagging surrounding heating pipes, close to where he worked. The lagging had been disturbed by workman, on numerous occasions over a fifteen year period, some thirty to forty years ago. He'd been exposed to the killer fibres and had unfortunately developed mesothelioma, an aggressive form of lung cancer for which there is no cure.

"Get the bill done, Kim, and get the client's damages to him ASAP. I'll give you a one-off bonus for all your efforts on the case."

"Promises, promises," Kim said, her eyes lighting up.

Spire started sifting through his post. "I'll check for any urgent stuff and get it done. Anything I don't finish I'll leave on my desk for you to deal with," he said, giving Kim a wink.

Kim rolled her eyes. "Yes, boss. So where are you off next on your UFO quest?"

"Heading back to London tomorrow morning for a briefing with GLENCOM, and then I'm probably flying over to the States, Nevada, to continue Lazarus' quest, as you eloquently put it," he smiled.

"So I" assume you'll be in need of my amazing cat feeding services again," Kim said, wandering back to her desk.

"I will certainly need your sterling cat-sitting services, if you're not too busy. It will probably be for ten days or so mind," Spire said, looking up from the mail.

CHAPTER 31

THE FOLLOWING DAY, Spire caught the early morning train to London – via Cardiff – arriving in Paddington at just after midday. He'd done enough driving this week and still felt a little too tired for another long drive. He moved through the commuters and tourists, far less than there normally was pre-Covid. He descended the stairs to the tube, passing an Evening Standard newspaper seller, the stand sporting the headline;

UFO's BUZZ U.S. MILITARY NAVY SHIPS OFF
CALIFORNIAN COAST

Thirty minutes later, Spire jumped off the tube at Vauxhall underground, made his way along Albert Embankment, and then down the alleyway alongside MI6 headquarters. He repeated the security procedure required to gain access and entered the Operations Room, lit by the familiar soft blue glow from the full Earth hologram.

"Ah, afternoon, Robert, good to see you. I'm sorry you've had a fraught couple of days," Dr Oliver Mathews said, getting up from in front of a monitor to greet him.

"Yes, my own fault, I should never have gone off-piste and ventured down there I guess, but it's good to be back," Spire said, shaking Mathews' outstretched hand.

"How was your journey up?

"Without incident I'm happy to say," Spire said, smiling, as he followed Dr Mathews over to the array of large screens that ran along the front of the room, the usual data and telemetry streaming down the screens from multiple global environmental crisis zones.

"Oh, whilst I remember," Mathews suddenly said, somewhat excitedly, "Come and take a look at this."

Spire followed the portly Dr Mathews across the operations room, to a far corner, where a few technicians - dressed in white overalls - were crouched down, fiddling with something on the floor.

"I know you've seen this little gadget before, but we're in the process of upgrading it," Mathews said, as they approached the group.

"Which gadget might this be?" Spire asked, as they reached the three guys in white lab coats.

"Our tech team have been working on the upgrades for a good while. It's the portable hologram generator, but now waterproof and with a few more 'stock' holograms added for your latest mission," Oliver said, grinning.

"Oh, I see," Spire said, somewhat confused.

"Good morning both," one of the tech guys said, looking up from what he was doing. "Sorry, can we just move back ten feet or so," he said, as he pressed a button on a small black remote device he was holding. As he did, a blue light lit up on the small black box on the floor. Five seconds or so ticked by, then suddenly a mass of billions of tiny molecules started to appear in front of them, suspended in mid-air about ten feet off the ground.

Spire stepped back, in awe, as always by the realism of the hologram materialising in the space above them. Seconds later, a Great White shark appeared, swimming and twisting through the air in front of them.

"This is in addition to the Hammerhead that's still programmed in. The entire device is now waterproof, making the shark holograms potentially more...useful," the tech guy smirked.

"It looks fantastic, so real!" Spire whispered, as he walked around the swimming shark, admiring its muscular, sleek body and soulless, black eyes. There was no visible projection coming from the equipment, just a faint whir. As he walked in front of the black box, the image of the shark showed signs of interference, blinking a little, before the full image materialised again as he cleared the invisible beams being emitted from the device.

"And this really works underwater?" Spire asked.

"Sure does, but not so easy to demonstrate. The device has a small buoyancy attachment, which keeps it as suspended under the water. The remote will work from a hundred feet or so," the tech guy added.

"Useful for ensuring an underwater location was kept diver-free, I'm sure," Oliver said, chuckling.

"Astonishing," Spire said, passing his hand through the shark's large dorsal fin.

"So what else have you chaps been working on?" Mathew's asked.

The technician looked excitedly at Oliver and Spire in turn. "Well, having been briefed on what your latest mission relates to, we have added a few more images, my personal favourite being a very life-like flying saucer," he said.

"Flying saucer?" Oliver repeated.

"You know, a UFO. We based it on the classic saucer shape, well more crescent-shaped actually, like the disc supposedly seen by Kenneth Arnold and from the description of the one that crashed at Roswell."

"Allegedly crashed at Roswell," Spire added.

The tech guy glanced at him and smiled. "Yes, of course."

"Well, let's see it," Mathews said, impatiently.

"Ah, could you give us ten minutes please sir, we need to make one more software tweak to make it perfect."

"Of course, come on Robert, we can see it on the way out. All this excitement, I forgot to mention, a good friend of yours is waiting for us in the meeting room. I just want to give you both a very quick briefing before you leave for the states."

Spire was taken off-guard, wondering who Oliver was referring to. They both headed into the meeting room, and sitting there, for his first visit to GLENCOM was Travis

Dexter, dressed smartly, but casual in a sports jacket, blue shirt and chinos.

"Come on Robert, what took you so long my friend?" Dexter joked, standing to shake Spire's hand. "I must admit, Oliver here has given me a very quick tour of the facility here, but I'm massively impressed, it's awesome," he said.

"Well you kept today's meeting quiet, but it's about time you paid a visit," Spire said, smiling.

"I called Travis in personally as soon as I knew he was coming over. Thought we should meet seeing as he was in London and considering he's accompanied you on so many missions, and helped enormously on most of them. I, we owe him a debt of gratitude," Oliver acknowledged.

Dexter shrugged. "Pleasure has been all mine. I'd have done it for free...well almost," he joked.

Oliver looked at Dexter over the rims of his glasses. "That can be arranged if you insist," he said.

Dexter parted his arms. "Second thoughts, my skills might be affected if I wasn't being compensated," he said, glancing at Spire.

"We'd better stick to the current arrangements then," Oliver said, smiling.

"So what's up?" Spire asked, changing the subject.

"Well, going back to the reason we're all here – the Lazarus assassination and suggestion that secret technologies and their origins are being hidden from the world; there's been a development. Our intel has confirmed that a rabbi, one Neil Gregorius was murdered yesterday in Budapest."

Spire looked at Dexter, and then back at Oliver. "And this murder is...connected?" he asked.

Oliver looked up at them from his computer screen. "His death was particularly nasty, symbolic almost. A noose was put around his neck and he was thrown over the *Elizabeth Bridge*, which spans the Danube."

"Did he drown?" Spire asked

"No, the killer made sure the rope wasn't long enough to hit the water."

"Ah, poor chap," Spire added.

"God-damn coward, son-of-a-bitch," Dexter added, a little less eloquently.

"Quite," Oliver said. British Intelligence confirms that a unit of the Hungarian Special Police searched the rabbi's apartment after and found a diary which mentioned a meeting between him, two other scholars, and Lazarus shortly before his death. The three scholars had been attending a religious event in Montenegro."

"Of course," Spire said, recalling that Lazarus in his presentation confirmed he'd met with three prominent religious scholars. "Lazarus said he'd met with three men of God, Christianity, Judaism and Islam when giving his presentation."

Spire then recalled the call that he and Isobel had received on the assassin's cell phone when they were in the café right after Lazarus' murder. "The assassin's phone; did you managed to unblock it?" he asked Oliver.

Oliver nodded. "We managed to get some data off it. Messages between one, Rabbi Neil Gregorius in Budapest, presumably the poor chap who was thrown off the bridge, a Bishop Valente, Montenegrin and Rome codes used, and one Dr Amjad Madani, who I assume is the Islamic scholar, again, Montenegrin codes and a code for an area just outside Delhi used."

"Clearly Dr Madani and this, Valente character are in danger, although it sounds like the bishop may well be behind Lazarus' death," Spire said.

Oliver sighed. "That's true. Let me think about those two. Clearly your priority is to get over to the States, see if you can find out what Lazarus was about to reveal. I'll send an update on the religious connection as soon as I can."

"Very well," Spire said.

"Oh, there's one more thing," Oliver said, sliding a white business card over the table towards them. "Travis gave me this; he found it in the wallet of one of the military thugs down in Rendlesham. GLENCOM will do some digging on the DOE and its potential link with this so called; *Project Aquarius,* and I'll update you on anything we find."

"Great," Spire said, looking at Dexter.

"Thank you for your hospitality today sir," Dexter said.

"No problem gentlemen. I suggest you go out and have a drink, savour your free time. You'll be jetting off tomorrow morning to the States to continue Lazarus' quest. You both realise of course that any discoveries, if they are as Lazarus stated, could be...Earth shattering."

Spire nodded. "Let's not jump to conclusions, but we can cross that bridge if we ever get to it."

Dexter slapped Spire on the back. "Come on Rob, you heard Oliver. Let's go and get a drink. Plan the start of our trip."

"Great idea," he said, getting up. He nodded to Oliver. "Until next time then."

"Oh, almost forgot. Let's go see if the tech team have sorted out the hologram. You need to take the device with you Robert. It's saved your life on a few occasions now."

The three of them headed out and over to where the three tech guys were standing around talking.

"Is it ready?" Oliver asked.

The tech guy turned as he heard Oliver's voice. "Ah, yes sir, give me a minute," he said, nodding to his two colleagues who headed straight for the box on the floor in order to change the setting. "Here," he said, handing the small remote to Spire. "You can do the honours, but it won't be as impressive in this confined space," he added.

Spire took the remote and gave Oliver and Travis a pensive look before pressing the button.

The three of them looked on in stunned silence as a forty-foot silvery / gun metal-grey craft appeared to hover five feet off the ground in front of them, it's form enveloping the desks and computer screens within the Ops Room, including most of the real Earth hologram at the far end.

"Wow!" Dexter commented.

The classic disc-shaped craft appeared to sway, ever so slightly, which added to its realism and blue, green and red lights strobed around the bottom of the disc in a hypnotic rhythm – blue, green, red and intense white, then back to blue again. Apart from that, the craft was seamless. The only markings Spire could see were what appeared to be black hieroglyphics, spanning the upper section of the craft.

"Jeez, it looks so real," Spire said, a large grin forming across his face. "What are those markings up there," he pointed.

The tech guy shrugged. "No idea, they are totally made up. We copied the hieroglyphs from witness testimony from the Roswell incident and also what the airmen supposedly saw on the craft that landed in Rendlesham Forest. Not bad eh?"

Spire shook his head. "Simply amazing," he said.

Oliver snapped the pair of them out of their trances. "Make sure that's ready for Robert to take with him in five minutes."

"Oh, yes...yes of course sir," the tech guy said, as Spire handed him back the tiny remote.

The hovering UFO fizzled out in front of their eyes, the Ops Room returning to normal once again.

"Thanks, guys," Oliver said. He looked at Spire and Dexter. "Ok, Robert, back to business. I'll have Amy post all the necessary information you need, for your trip, on your secure website. As usual, if there's anything you require to get the mission done, just give me a shout."

"Of course," Spire smiled.

The tech guy approached and handed Spire a neat black leather case with a strap. "There you go. All the instructions are in there, including the buoyancy attachment. Please take care of it," he said.

"Is the Pope a Catholic?" Oliver said, raising his eyebrows.

The tech guy smiled and walked back over to his two colleagues.

"You both take care, and Travis, make sure you get him back in one piece."

"Count on it, Oliver."

"Report back to me on the usual basis Robert," Oliver said, as the three of them headed for the exit...

The End of Part 2

"I know other astronauts share my feelings.... And we know the government is sitting on hard evidence of UFOs."
-- Astronaut, Gordon Cooper

Spire Returns in the final part of the trilogy;

The Galileo Conspiracy - Part 3: Disclosure

Order Now!

Read Chapter 1 below

References, Credits and Further Research Suggestions

Whilst The Galileo Project is a work of fiction, inspiration for the novel has come from multiple sources listed and credited below. The recent release by the Pentagon of the U.S. Navy 'UFO' gun-camera UFO footage, and mystery triangular craft filmed with night-vision buzzing U.S. warships off San Diego and acknowledgement of there being a secretly funded AATIP - Advanced Aerospace Threat Identification program, set up with the purpose of investigated the UFO / UAP (unidentified aerial phenomenon)

*This **alleged** UFO threat is a major new development in the UFO phenomenon, coupled with recent documentaries and soon-to-be released documentaries and movies on the subject such as, SIRIUS,*

UNACKNOWLEDGED and Dr Stephen Greer's and UFO historian, Richard Dolan's (name may sound familiar!) relentless pursuit of UFO disclosure. Recent documentaries such as those above and, THE PHENOMENON (which provides a historical to date view on the subject) and soon-to-be-released, CAPEL GREEN, which deals with the U.K.'s Rendlesham Forest Incident are 'must see' movies for anyone interested in this subject.

There is also the UAP report which will be presented to the Pentagon on June 2021, which by all accounts will acknowledge the reality of UFO's flying about the world's skies...

Credits

1. *Pen Y Fan summit photo – Summitornothing.co.uk*
2. *Possible nuclear bunker site Little Haven – Google Maps*
3. *John Petts UFO sighting – Market Business News – Swansea UFO*
4. *Lt. Colonel Charles Halt - Rendlesham Audio Tape December 1980- Soundcloud.com*
5. *UFO landing spot image – Google Maps*
2. *RAF Woodbridge East Gate Photo- Wikipedia*
3. *Bob Lazar, Area 51 and Flying saucers – general references*
4. *Broad Haven children's UFO pictures – BBC News, Broad Haven UFO sightings marked 40 years on*
8. *The Rendlesham Forest UFO photo – Atlas Obscura photo*
9. *Existence of alleged alien Moon base -Former US Air Force Sergeant,*
Karl Wolfe (now deceased)
10. *Richard Dolan – Author / Lecturer and UFO historian / expert*
11. *Photos of Haven Fort Hotel and other West Wales locations taken by the author, Simon Rosser.*
12. *Shag Harbour UFO incident – October 1967*

CHAPTER 1

Nevada, USA

SPIRE GLANCED OUT of the window down onto the great Utah Salt Lakes, a part of the journey some three quarters of flight time through; vast puddles of white against the parched dry land some 33,000 feet below. Twenty four hours earlier, he and Travis had left GLENCOM and gone for a few early beers and a nice steak near to his apartment in Russel Square.

As Spire looked down, the authoritative voice of the captain drifted out from the aircraft's tannoy system. "This is Captain Avalon here. Just a quick word from the cockpit to let you know we are currently cruising at 33,000 feet, with a speed of just under 680 knots. The weather is going to hold for us all the way over to Nevada. If you're sitting in a window seat you'll have a great view of Utah's salt lakes below. I'll not disturb you again until our approach into McCarran, in about two hours. Enjoy the rest of your flight."

Dexter, who'd been snoring next to Spire, opened his eyes. "Did I miss something?"

"No, just the pilot giving an update, apologising to the passengers for the person in seat thirty-four who's been snoring like a bear."

Dexter opened his eyes. "You're kidding right. Jeez, sorry about that."

"I think it's time for another gin and tonic," Spire said, pressing the button on the entertainment system to call the flight attendant.

Rosie, who'd been serving in business class the entire flight, appeared a few moments later.

"What can I get you guys?" she asked.

"A gin and tonic for me, and maybe another sleeping tonic for my friend – oh, and some more nuts please."

"Make it a beer instead, please, Rosie," Dexter said.

"Sounds better than sleeping tonic," Rosie replied, smiling.

Three more drinks each and another hour or two later and the Sierra Nevada Mountains came into view.

"Did you know the Sierra's had the largest tree in the world?"

"Really?" Spire said.

"*General Sherman*, a giant sequoia. They reckon it's around 2300-2700 years old."

"No way, that's incredible!"

Dexter continued. "And also *Lake Tahoe*, which is the largest alpine lake in North America and not to mention *Mount Whitney*, at 14,505 feet, the highest point in the U.S.A."

Now clear of the mountain range, the pale yellow of the Nevada Desert fanned out in all direction below. Spire looked down, wondering where Area 51 was located. He contemplated if he and Dexter could get anywhere near America's most guarded and elusive base - an area known as S-4 / Groom Lake. *Could Lazarus' claims be true?* Was the U.S. Government reverse-engineering alien craft there together with the literally out-of-this-world, anti-gravity propulsion technology that powered them, and had it been in American hands since the late 1950's? Could it be, that top secret, U.S. Military Industrial Complex technology, is being tested against its own U.S. Navy by flying their advanced craft close to U.S. warships, to perhaps test, and even attempt to fool them that genuine other-worldly visitors were watching. Or was it a foreign power, or indeed genuine aliens?

Spire had no idea, but recent videos which had surfaced did suggest that there were highly advanced craft buzzing U.S. Navy warships and were being seen by multiple witnesses. *Could these be the craft Lazarus was working on, talking about?* Spire pondered the possibilities of such technology being able to revolutionise the world, provide free alternative energy, and solve the global warming crisis that the world continued to sleepwalk in to.

The seat belt signs pinged on, dragging Spire from his thoughts on the UFO phenomenon, followed by the captain's voice. "Cabin crew, thirty minutes until we start our descent into McCarran."

Spire rubbed his eyes. The flight had been good. "That last hour and a half zipped by," he said to Dexter.

"Sure did, buddy. Feels good to be home," he said.

The 747 glided effortlessly down, landing with a solid *thud* as the aircraft's four Rolls-Royce RB211-524Gs went into reverse thrust to slow the jet, as air from the engine's fans was deflected out of the side of the engine, creating massive drag.

Spire stretched. "Always felt good to be back on solid ground."

Off the aircraft and finally out of the terminal building, Spire let the warm afternoon sun wash over his face for a few moments as he followed Dexter to the minicab zone. The time was 2.45 p.m. local time. They walked along the terminal building, passing multiple taxi zones for all the different casino resorts, before joining a short queue for the Flamingo Resort.

Dexter signalled, and a white and black cab pulled over. "Howdy guys. Where ya going?" the driver asked, as he jumped out and helped them both with their luggage.

"We're good. Heading to the Flamingo buddy," Dexter said."

"Jump in. You guys here for business or pleasure?"

"Little bit of both," Spire replied.

"Well, there's plenty of pleasure to be had here, that's for sure!" the driver said, pulling the cab out of the airport and onto Paradise Road for the short drive to the main Las Vegas strip.

After a ten minute drive along the interstate the *MGM Grand* appeared on their right, followed by the *New York-New York Hotel and Casino.* The cab then turned left off the interstate and onto Frank Sinatra Drive, passing *The Excalibur* and finally onto the *Flamingo.*

"Here ya go guys, have a lucky stay here in Vegas."

The driver had no idea. "We'll certainly need plenty of that," Spire joked, handing him the fare, plus a ten dollar tip.

"Home sweet home," Dexter said, looking up at the casino.

Spire shook his head and laughed. "It amuses me that you stay here so often."

"Not often enough," Dexter replied.

They both headed into the cool air-conditioned foyer of the casino and Spire checked in amidst the constant hum and melodies coming from the slot machines just off the main foyer.

"Welcome back Mr Dexter," the female concierge said, smiling. "And you enjoy your stay too Mr Spire," she added, as she handed Spire his key card.

"You're on the tenth floor. I'm five above you. Let's grab a few hours of rest to recover from the flight, and meet in the lobby at say, six p.m." Dexter said, as they headed over to the bank of elevators.

"Perfect," Spire said, as the elevator door *pinged* open on the tenth.

Once in his room, Spire quickly unpacked, making sure that the special equipment given to him by GLENCOM was still intact. He then hid it away under the bed. He opened and powered up his laptop and signed into the GLENCOM secure site and sent a brief message to Oliver, confirming they'd both checked in and that he'd report back in more detail once he had any further useful information. There were no messages waiting for him.

He sent a message to both Kim and Isobel, had a shower and sank back onto the bed to grab a few hours rest before meeting up with Dexter again. It sure was going to be an interesting evening. *A bit of fun was needed before starting the serious work tomorrow*, Spire thought.

To be continued....

The Galileo Project: Disclosure (Part 3) is out in October 2021 and can be pre-ordered HERE

Also by the same author;
(Click the universal book links below)

Robert Spire Thriller Series

Tipping Point – Spire 1
Impact Point – Spire 2
Melt Zone – Spire 3
Cataclysm of the Ancients – Spire 4
Crypto – Spire 5
Box Set -Spire Thrillers 1- 4

Salient – Sci-Fi Mystery Thriller
Red Mist – Fast Paced Espionage Thriller
Amber Lee Sci-Fi Alien Invasion Adventures –
Vaporized and Vaporized ll

Please visit the Author's Website and sign up for the author's newsletter and FREE e-books. Scroll down to download your FREE copy of Tipping Point now.